PUBLISHED BY Kol Anderson

Copyright © Cover design Kol Anderson 2016

Copyright © Kol Anderson 2016

Amazon Edition

This eBook is licensed for your personal enjoyment only. This eBook may not be resold or given away to other people. If you would like to share this book with another person, please purchase an additional copy for each recipient. If you're reading this book and did not purchase it, or it was not purchased for your use only, then please return to amazon.com and purchase your own copy. Thank you for respecting the hard work of this author.

© 2016 KOL ANDERSON

EDITOR: DIANE NELSON

Happy Birthday, Lu.
Xoxo

As always a HUGE thanks to everyone who helped, supported, reviewed my works, and still continue to do so, everyone who shared a link, or told their friends, everyone who joined the street team and helped keep me motivated. A special thank you to Louis Stevens, Amanda Eisenthal, Daniela Reika, Jen Boltz, Scott Burkett and Bev Sutherland for all their help and for making this release possible.

I love and cherish you guys from the bottom of my heart.

A very special thanks to Diane Nelson for editing the manuscript!
Thank you for all your help, babe!

1
COLTON

It was dark.

The kind of dark that unleashed every monster and brought to life every nightmare you'd ever buried. Staying in the dark seemed like a terrible idea but not quite as terrible as what was in store for me back in that cell. And then there was a thunderstorm, and it started to rain. The downpour was so heavy I couldn't breathe. I'd stopped running. The branches from trees had given me new wounds to worry about and after that sudden burst of adrenaline I'd experienced back at the house, my body was now in even more pain and I was unable to move, paralyzed from panic or pain. It was anyone's guess.

It looked like this was the end of the line.

Any minute now, my captors would find me and I would be thrown back into that hell. It was obvious things would be worse this time. I should have known that would be the outcome of my stupid little escape attempt. I cowered behind a tree, shaking uncontrollably, partly because of the cold and partly from fear. I could hear my teeth chattering, the rain falling on my body, and I was drenched. My bare feet were raw from being scraped over broken tree branches and tiny gravels, and God knows what else, during the extremely short-lived endeavor of running through that endless forest.

Footsteps crunched on the wet ground. They made their way through the dirt and then someone shone a flashlight a few feet away from where I was hiding. "Come on, Colton," I heard Logan's voice. "You can't hide forever. But you can lessen your punishment!"

I felt like even my lungs were making a noise as loud as the thunderstorm, so I held my breath because I knew Logan was lying. The punishment, this time, would be something much worse than I could even dream of. I was certain of that. Certain that I was about to be killed by a bunch of idiots and I didn't even know why. I didn't even know how I'd survived that long, let alone take anything they were planning for me now that I had tried to flee. The scenarios that went through my head—of what was about to happen, because sure enough, I was going to get caught, even I knew that—robbed me of my breath. So I tried to stay hidden even though I knew my number was up, for however long that lasted.

I felt something grab my shoulder in the dark, a hand or a claw. Strong arms grabbed me and dragged me away from the tree, and hauled me through the forest, through the same tree branches that sliced into my skin and the same gravel that wounded my feet until we reached a clearing, and that's when I was pushed to the ground.

Everything around me was thick, dense mud.

I lifted my head to see. There were bright lights shining in my face and I couldn't see their faces. Inside, I knew it was them but denial sounded a lot better than accepting that my life had reached its end. For all the paralyzing fear that I had fought back while I was hiding, I felt completely numb now. No fear, just acceptance, and the need to get to the end so this could all be over. But the faces remained behind the veil of the lights for a long time and maybe that was to mess with me or because they themselves knew this fact and wanted it to last as much as I wanted it to end.

One of them finally brought their flashlight and stepped forward. "Well then, people," Devyn said. "Looks like we're about to end this chapter sooner than we thought we would."

I truly thought I could accept it. The fact that I was going to die or that I was going to die without seeing Jason. There are things in life you take for granted because it's the only way you can get through life without having constant panic attacks. If it was up to me, I'd never leave Jason's side but that's not how it works. In this world, there are rules that can't be broken. But none of it mattered now. I just prayed they had the decency to give Jason my remains so he could cremate me and throw my ashes all over Europe. So he could have the closure that I was being denied. But I was through begging them. Not just because they weren't going to listen but also because I was drained. Inside, I had given up. Pretty sure I almost wanted to die at their hands. Maybe it was all the torture they'd put me through and the fact that I could no longer take any more of it, or maybe it was the darkness inside me that wanted it. I could see myself dying. I could see my life ending and the pain ending right along with it. I was looking forward to not feeling a thing. The only thing that hurt worse than all the pain they had inflicted on me was Jason's absence. I wanted to see him one last time but I knew that was never going to happen. I knew they would never allow it. I knew that would be their final blow, the last round of torture.

"Did you really think you could outrun us?" Devyn laughed. I know he was trying to get to me but it wasn't working. Any sense of winning or losing had long since been extracted out of me. I no longer felt insulted or humiliated. Their words were just words. They had no impact. The place where my heart used to be was empty. I might have looked and breathed like an actual person existed inside me, but I knew that wasn't true. I felt that void, the vacuum where a human had lived once, and I felt the vast emptiness of my soul, dragging me into the murky, bottomless swamp that was my end.

I may have felt grief, terror and panic, any of those emotions but, instead, I felt nothing. When Logan lifted his nightstick and started beating me with it, I felt like they were pulling me back in the world of the living. The first time he swung the thing it hit me right in the ribs, leaving me coughing up blood. I actually felt those ribs cracking under the weight of the stick, felt the weight of my body becoming hard for my chest to hold up, making me double over and puke blood and bile all over the muddy ground. Logan raised the stick and swung again, and this time, the heavy end of the stick was laid into my back and it knocked the wind out of me. I fell to the ground on my face. There was no getting away. There was nowhere to run. Nowhere to go. This small clearing in the forest was all I had and they surrounded me like an invisible fence. I tried to get up, using my hands to carry my weight, but out of nowhere, I felt the stick colliding with my skull. The hit almost severed my connection with the world. Logan grabbed my hair and forced me to get up, so I scrambled to get on my knees. When I stared up at him, blood made way into my eyes from my hair and I blinked it off, but it kept coming back, thicker and more profusely.

"That's what you get for trying to run," Logan said, spitting on my face.

Devyn came to check on me and placed a finger along my neck to check my pulse. I don't know what he found, but he stood and I watched Grey grabbing me and pulling me up. But he may as well have been pulling up a lifeless corpse.

"Looks like we fucked him up good," Grey said. "He won't even struggle."

With that he pushed me back to the ground and the rain was getting inside my nose and my mouth making it hard for me to breathe. I should have moved away but I didn't. I lay there until Grey was on top of me. "Don't think we're going to let you off the hook just because we have to kill you now," he said. "What do you say, Colton? One last fuck for old times' sake?"

His hand grabbed my jaw and I grabbed his hand or tried to because my grip went slack. I could feel tears streaming down my face, but they got mixed with the cold rainwater, and I could see him ready to hurt me again, but I couldn't do a thing to stop him. The effort was too much for my body and for my spirit. Grey turned me over on the ground and my face was forced into the mud, and when I tried to move my head, I saw the switchblade. It was the same one Grey had used on me several times, to torture me. It was almost within my reach but I made no effort to pick it up. Grey lowered my pants and assaulted my body one more time but I didn't struggle. The only movement my body made was in response to Grey's thrusts. It was painful but I wasn't completely conscious. Something inside me was broken, but I had no idea what and I didn't care.

Not even about Jason.

If he found me now, I wasn't even sure what he would find.

What I was now, you couldn't call that alive.

Jason was better off without it.

As was the rest of the world.

Grey stopped.

I felt his warm cum, dripping, finding a way out of my body and it made me sick.

My eyes were starting to close.

I tried to keep them open.

The blade was still in view.

Grey still hadn't noticed it. No one had.

They were too busy playing with a corpse to know they were missing a weapon.

"What the hell was that?" It was Ash. I realized they noticed something, a sound perhaps, that had them alarmed, but the pattering of the rain and the sound of their feet sloshing about in the mud was all I heard. *Why am I not dead yet?*

"Shit," Devyn said, alarmed. "That's Jason's car."

"How do you know?" Grey asked. I could hear the sounds of cars approaching now too, honking and making crunching noises in the gravel and rain as they moved toward us. Then there were lights, brighter than the flashlights, also approaching.

"How did they find us?"

"How the fuck should I know?" Devyn snapped. "What're we going to do now? He's not alone! There's a fucking army with him!"

"Run," Grey said.

"What?" Devyn and the others didn't seem willing to leave their friend.

"Don't let them catch you," Grey said. "Devyn, just do as I say! I'll catch up!"

"What about him?" Devyn was clearly talking about me.

"I'll handle him," Grey said. "Now leave!"

I heard them all running, and then before Grey could grab me again, I grabbed the blade and jabbed it at his face. In my head, all I could think was *Jason's here.* The flashlight dropped from Grey's hand and in its light, I saw him howling and holding a hand to one side of his face. When he lowered that hand, the blade was still lodged inside the bleeding, pus-dripping mass of flesh.

He screamed even louder and grabbed the free end of the blade and pulled it out of his eye. He looked inhuman. He tossed the knife aside and pulled me up, and I felt the muzzle of a gun pressing into my temple as he grabbed me from behind and held me in a stranglehold.

There were people walking through the thicket, being slowed down by the rain but still continuing to walk. Grey's screaming must have led them right to us.

They were carrying their own flashlights but I saw something else—weapons—serious rifles and firearms of every caliber I could see out there in the hands of those men. Devyn was right. It was an army. At first, I thought it was a joke Grey and the others were playing on me, that this had to be another game, and they wanted me to feel for a few minutes that I had a chance at life just to take it away the next moment. But as the footsteps came closer, the faces started to get familiar.

Until I saw one that made me want to run toward him.

"Jason!" I screamed and my voice was hoarse and barely audible in the rain. But Grey's hold on me was tighter now. All I wanted was to be close to Jason one last time, feel his chest against my face and his strong arms around me, but Grey wouldn't let me.

"Grey we've got you surrounded," Jason said and it seemed strange to me that Jason knew his name. "The house too. There's nowhere to run. You have to surrender and put an end to this."

Grey spit at him. "No one's going to surrender," he said. "Least of all me. If I go down, your brother goes down with me."

It was too dark to see the emotions on Jason's face but he didn't move from where he was which meant the danger wasn't over. "Your beef is with me. Do you want to take out your anger? Get your revenge?" Jason threw his arms in the air. "Take me. My brother's done nothing to deserve this."

"No," Grey said and, still keeping my body close to his, he pushed me to the ground on my knees.

This time, the gun was at the back of my head. "Maybe he hasn't done anything to deserve this," Grey said, "but you sure as hell have. And the best way to hurt you is to hurt him. I know that now, Hamilton."

"This isn't fair."

"Neither was what you did to my brother!" Grey yelled. For the first time, I heard something other than cruelty in his voice. It was pain. Like there was when he was talking about his brother dying back in the house. Like there was in Jason's voice right now.

"I didn't kill your brother to hurt you," Jason said. "I did it because he was a threat to us. You know the business we're in. You know, Grey, because you were part of it once. You know if someone comes on your turf and threatens the life of your family, you have no choice but to end that person's life."

That's when I realized a part of me had wanted Jason to deny it. Deny that he had a hand in killing someone, let alone someone's family. I mean, I'm not stupid, I know my brother and uncle are into some shady stuff but murder? I couldn't believe my ears. My brother wasn't capable of killing someone, it wasn't true. Maybe Jason was covering for someone. Like, Uncle Dave. Pretty sure Dave was capable of anything.

"I don't care why you did it," Grey said. "And your rationalizations might have been great at Robbie's funeral, but you didn't even have the decency to give back his body."

"I had nothing to do with that," Jason said. "My uncle took care of it but, still, I'm saying sorry. Just end this here and we can all go back to our lives. I gave your brother that choice, to just walk away but he didn't listen.

Now I'm going to give you that same option. Tell me you're smarter than him. *Please*, tell me you're smarter than some guy who walked into my place of business and threatened my brother's life."

"It's too late for apologies," Grey said. "This little shit is going to die! Because I want to see you feel the same pain that I went through."

"You hurt my brother and I swear to God you will never get out of here alive."

Grey laughed. "You think I give a shit about dying?"

For the split second in which I heard Grey cocking that gun and it being pressed into my skull, I felt the whole world go still.

There was a scuffle, someone trying to get Grey to stop, and the metal of the gun was no longer hard-pressed into my cranium. I could hear Grey struggling behind me with someone, probably one of Jason's army, and I felt them scrambling to win in the pouring rain and mud, and I looked up at Jason. The distance between us was barely a few feet and Jason was already ending it by running toward me. I knew I was going to break the minute he touched me and I was looking forward to it. The emptiness was slowly fading and I was starting to feel things again, my absolute love for Jason and the intense craving to be in his arms… a loud bang reverberated, followed by another, and I saw Jason, still coming toward me, but time was going slow and everything inside my head was as thick as the mud and slosh around me. Jason grabbed me and I felt him lifting my shirt, and I couldn't understand why until I saw the blood pouring from an open wound in my chest… My face hit Jason's shoulder…

And that's when everything went silent.

2
JASON

I held him in my arms when he fell unconscious on my shoulder.

It couldn't be true, I'd just saved him! I'd done everything in my power to do it… there was no way I was accepting the fact that something had happened to him. But my brother had just suffered a gunshot wound and that wasn't something you could take lightly. God only knew what other damage they had done to him, but now Grey had tried to shoot him dead. I realized, as I placed Colton gently on the ground, that if I had come so much as a minute late, my brother might not have been alive at all. I checked his wound and there was so much blood I couldn't even think straight. I saw evidence of a recent beating, severe bruising around his ribs and in the distance I noticed a nightstick lying a few feet away from us.

"How far is the nearest hospital?" I asked Gary who was standing behind me, waiting for my instructions.

"With the way I drive," Gary said. "Not far."

"Even if by some miracle he survives the bullet," Grey said from where he was being held down by one of Gary's men. "He's not going to survive Logan's beating, we made sure of that."

I forced myself to get up.

The men watched my every move, and I'm sure they had no idea what was going on when I grabbed that nightstick from the ground and brought it toward Grey. "This is what you used to beat him?" I asked. The men realized my intention and left Grey's side, giving me enough space so I could swing the stick at Grey. With one single blow, Grey was doubled over and spewing blood. I held out the stick to one of the men. "Hold on to this," I said and went back to Colton.

"You Hamiltons," Grey said. "You think you're such big shots. But I just raped your brother bloody and beat him up and there was nothing you could do."

For Colton's sake, I had to ignore Grey at that moment.

"Sir," one of the men said, "what would you like us to do with him?"

"Keep him here," I said. "Until further orders."

"I killed your brother, Jason. You have to shoot me!" Grey yelled.

I got up and walked up to them. "If he tries to run, break his legs," I said to the men. "But keep him alive at all costs. If I find him dead when I get back, I'll stick the two of you in the same grave as him."

I walked back to my brother and let Grey be dragged by the men and permitted him to yell things at me. I picked Colton up, and Gary and the others walked with me to where our cars were parked. Colton wasn't moving but he was breathing. I was alarmed by the amount of weight he'd lost since the last time we were together. I placed him in the back of my SUV and got in with him while Gary stepped into the driver's seat.

Gary pressed the device to his ear and answered a call. After a while, he hung up and turned to me. "One of the guys just called," he said. "They found the others. What do you want them to do?"

Everything raced through my mind at once. "Keep them all inside the house," I told Gary. "No one escapes. And they should be kept alive. That's important, Gary."

Gary relayed the information to his men and we started to drive. All the way to the hospital I kept my composure even though all I wanted was to break down. "And Gary," I said, "anyone asks, we found Colton outside of Fairview. There was no sign of the kidnappers. We simply never heard from them again."

"Of course, Jason."

"Where's Dave?"

"Dave said he was driving to the hospital ahead of us," Gary said. "He knows someone there, maybe they can help keep all this under wraps."

"It won't be possible to keep this under wraps," I said. "But we can make sure no one gets wind of this, what really happened or who brought Colton back."

"I understand."

"Gary," I said, "thanks for all your help."

"Please don't thank me," Gary said. "Your father helped me and my family when I was in need. The least I can do is to return the favor."

"It's strange."

"What is, sir?"

"The whole world thinks my father's a monster."

Gary paused. He changed the gear and then spoke again. "Sometimes we have no choice but to be monsters to some," he said. "So we can be angels to the rest. Your father had a following, Jason. Don't ever doubt the loyalty he instilled in people. You're the same. Colton might look like his father, but you're the one protecting his legacy, you're the one taking care of the family. Your father would have been proud of you."

I wondered if Gary knew.

Or if he did, how much.

Did he know that my brother and I were partners? That we loved each other in ways that were impossible to understand, sinful to even fathom? That what bound us wasn't some mere sibling connection but undying, interminable love? That we were practically married? Would my father still be proud if he knew? Would these people still follow me to hell and back if they knew I had every intention of running and leaving the business with Dave? That if it wasn't for Colton's kidnapping, we would have been far away right now? No worries, no crime syndicate, no death, no hidden cache carrying weapons that could end wars? Or begin them?

Of course not.

Gary had no clue that the legacy he thought I was protecting was in fact forced on me when I was still in high school, and I had no intention of carrying it forward. It was this legacy that had put Colton in danger in the first place. If it wasn't for the family business, I wouldn't be in this mess and neither would my innocent little brother. Grey was wrong. Neither of us had done anything to deserve this but here we were—facing war anyway.

It was a vicious cycle.

And someone had to put a stop to it.

I had a sinking feeling that someone was going to be me.

By the time we reached the hospital my anxiety had reached unbearable levels. It had stopped raining and as I carried Colton into the emergency room all kinds of scenarios kept flashing through my head. And then he was being taken away and even the small closeness I had felt to him was breaking, and I had no choice but to silently wait for the doctor's verdict.

After what seemed like centuries later, one of the doctors came and told me Colton would be in surgery for the next few hours, that he was in a coma because of the head injury and that they needed to operate right away.

They had me sign some forms and for the first time in my life, I signed those papers blindly. After that, there was nothing to do but wait.

My mind kept going back to all those times, every single time we had been together, and I wanted it all back. I wanted this whole thing to be a nightmare. I wanted to wake up and find Colton in my arms, in our bed, whining about stupid little things like bad sushi.

"Jason," Uncle Dave's voice broke my train of thought and I realized I was still in the waiting room.

"Hi."

Dave came to sit right next to me. "Sorry it took me so long," he said. "I was talking to a friend of mine. He's the Chief-of-Medicine and he assured me everything's going to be fine. They're going to give Colton the best treatment possible."

"It's been hours!" I snapped. "What the hell are they doing in there?"

"He'll be fine."

"You don't know that."

"He made it this far, didn't he?"

"You didn't see him, Dave. The way the doctors looked at me, I knew what they were thinking."

"What?"

"Don't make me say it out loud."

"If you can't say it out loud then you shouldn't be thinking it."

"Jason Hamilton?" A doctor wearing a surgical mask walked up to me and lowered the mask to talk.

It took all my strength to not go crazy as I stood and waited for him to speak. "That's me."

"Your brother's still comatose," the doctor said. "But we're doing all we can. The bullet wound was actually the least of our problems. The bullet barely grazed his organs. The real damage is from blunt trauma to his skull. It's caused some internal damage and bleeding. We're keeping him under observation. But we honestly won't know how much damage we're looking at until he wakes up."

"How long will that take?"

"In cases like this there's no way to know for sure," the doctor said. "But I think about two, three weeks."

"That doesn't sound so bad."

"He's going wake up from the coma," the doctor said. "But there's no way to tell how much damage there's going to be."

"What're the chances of there being zero damage?"

"None, I'd say. An injury that severe, we're probably looking at paralysis, or it could be a loss of some other faculty. I'm sorry Mr. Hamilton, I'm afraid I don't have any good news except for the fact that your brother's going to be alive."

He's going to be okay, I told myself. He didn't make it out alive to become a vegetable. Not that I'd love him any less if something did go wrong, I just couldn't imagine him facing something that harsh. I knew how much it would hurt him.

"There's one more thing," the doctor said. "In cases where there's sexual assault involved, we're obligated to take DNA samples to determine the identity of the offender. We're also giving him some preventive medication against common STDs but we're waiting on a blood serum test to determine if he's at risk for STIs. If you have any information regarding that, you should tell us. Every bit helps."

My mind wanted to block all of this but I had to stand there and listen instead.

"Thank you, Doctor," Dave said. "We all want to know who the perpetrator is." He placed a hand on my back. "My nephew's having a hard time, it being his brother and all. I hope you'll excuse him."

"Of course, I understand completely, Mr. Hamilton. I can imagine what you must be going through."

No, you can't.

"He's going to be fine," Dave said, the minute the doctor was gone. "But for a second there you looked like you were about to tell the doctor who the abuser is, Jason. Get a hold of yourself."

"I was never going to tell him."

"Well, it seemed like you might drop a hint. Anyway, you need to get some rest. I want you to go home, I'll be here and I'll let you know if the doctors have anything…"

"I'm not going anywhere."

"Jason, you haven't slept in days!"

"I'm *not* going anywhere."

"Fine. Then stay here. Kill yourself for all I care!"

Dave stormed out and I knew he was pissed, but I didn't care.

I'm afraid I don't have any good news except for the fact that your brother's going to be alive.

There was no way I was leaving this hospital until I knew he was going to be okay, until I heard him speak or saw him awake.

3

JASON

I'm not a religious person. I have no problem with people who hold their faith dear. In fact, in some weird way, I found my own comfort in seeing people find comfort in their god. I just could never give so much power, that much faith, away to an unknown entity. The only people you can trust wholly in my world are yourself and your family. Place your trust in anyone else and you end up on the ground next to the other fools who made that same mistake. Yet I found myself through the next forty-eight hours of my life seriously considering converting to some type of faith, as I held Colton's hand next to his hospital bed.

For a moment it didn't seem so bad to remove the burden I was carrying and give it to someone else to carry for a while. Have someone I could plead with for my brother's life. Give the weight of my crushing guilt and let them carry it. How easy that would be, putting your trust in a greater being than you and trusting it to fix everything wrong in this world.

But as I kissed Colton's bruised fingers and willed him to wake up from the darkness he was lost in, there was no doubt that I was my brother's only hope for getting through, just like he was mine. There was no one else who would help us. No one else gave a damn about us as much as we did. I had to be strong, I had to know what to do, I had to be the one to pull Colton through. I was willing my strength to flow through his fingers into his body and reach deep into his soul and wake him up. I needed him to respond to my touch like he used to when the mere whisper of my fingers against his soft skin would send shivers up his spine and make his pupils dilate in pleasure.

He had to wake up, and he had to be okay. I wouldn't accept anything less. We had a beautiful future ahead for us, one filled with beaches and planes and exotic locations and nights that never ended.

"Okay?" I whispered to him. "So you wake up. You wake up for me because I'm not even halfway through loving you."

"Sir?"

I kiss Colton's fingers again before looking up from the bed and into Gary's demure face.

"What is it?"

"The head nurse asked me to inform you they need to bathe Colton and change his sheets. She wanted me to ask you to give them the room."

"Why couldn't she ask me herself?"

"Apparently, sir, her nurses prefer not to speak to you after the last incident."

I smiled despite myself. After the scene I'd made at a nurse's indifferent treatment of Colton the day before, at least I knew my brother now had the dedicated attention of management behind his care.

"Come on, sir," Gary urged again. "I have some details to discuss with you anyway. Let's leave the nurses to do their jobs."

I nodded, giving Gary the acknowledgment he required, but didn't move. Instead, I picked up Colton's hand again, kissed his knuckles and then squeezed his fingers hard, letting him know through my touch that I'd be just outside the room and back shortly.

He looked so peaceful as I left him there, even with the healing bruises still discoloring his face. I walked past a pair of short nurses waiting at the door and I smiled disarmingly at them. The pair scowled at me, and Gary all but led me away from the room and down the hall. My small moment of mirth died when I recognized the look on Gary's face. It wasn't his usual detached expression. It was the "we've got the world's shit on our shoulders," look and it was the last thing I wanted to deal with right now.

"Out with it."

"I've been in constant contact with our men. One of them tried to escape. Ash, I believe."

"Did he succeed?"

"No, sir."

"Then why are you giving me that face?"

"Ash tried to escape by setting fire to the secret location. The whole compound burned down. All our men are fine, just some smoke inhalation. The guests made it out too, but they need medical attention."

The 'guests' were what they referred to captives in public, in the instance that anyone might be overhearing our conversation. Grey, Devyn, Logan, and Ash were anything but guests. They were our lifeline. My hate for them was what kept me going, and what kept me strong for Colton. The hate I felt for them was a tangible thing, I could touch it, and I held it close to my chest, nurturing it softly and letting it grow bigger every hour I spent watching Colton fight for his life.

"Your uncle wants to get involved now," Gary continued.

"Dave's got nothing to do with them," I said. "He does not get to take this away from me. Is that clear?"

Gary didn't answer other than giving me a curt nod. He was there for me and Colton, and I knew that. Gary was perhaps the only person, aside from Colton, that I knew would always give it to me straight, and that I could trust.

"Where are they now?"

"Location B, sir."

I nodded, my mind racing a million thousand miles per second. "That won't do for the long term." The thought of four captives and a six contingent army of private soldiers guarding them holed up in a two-bedroom apartment on the outskirts of town was as temporary as it got. Fuck. "We should activate the cottage. It's not finished yet, but it will do."

"My thoughts too, sir. I'll set the ball in motion."

At that moment the nurses walked out of Colton's room, and I was already up on my feet. "Gary? Don't update Dave just yet. Leave him to me, okay?"

"Done, sir."

With that, Gary left and I strolled back into the hospital room.

Colton had the face of a baby. I always teased him about that. Now that he was clean-shaven, I saw that baby face again. Despite the vicious bruises that still colored his complexion. He was beautiful, and despite his best efforts to make his face look manlier, he will always be my baby brother.

I loved seeing him looking clean and refreshed after his bath time; it made me happy. Maybe one day I would stop seeing him the way I'd found him, broken and covered in filth, and those memories would stop haunting me.

I wiped a wet tangle of hair from his forehead and tucked it behind his ear. It was difficult to do with the huge bandage covering most of his head, keeping his brain from falling off his head, but the gesture gave me comfort. What did Ash really think? That I would allow him to just run away and not face up to what they all did to him? They had to be crazier than I had thought.

Revenge. It was what fueled me and what fed me. Right now I was pigging out on it, using it to keep awake and to keep me alive. What I refused to think about was what would be there once the revenge was exacted. What would I have left? Would I be able to look Colton in the eyes again, or would the guilt never allow me to get that close to him again?

I sighed and resumed my vigil next to Colton's bed. No need to be thinking of that right now. I picked up Colton's hand and held it tight before I started telling him his favorite stories about our time growing up.

I had no idea what time it was when I shot awake, but my nerves were on edge and I felt someone hovering in the room. I spun around to see Dave standing in the door watching us wordlessly. Numb pain shot up my arm as I disentangled my arm from Colton's and slowly straightened my back. "You shouldn't hover, Uncle Dave."

Dave walked into the room. "You two look sweet together."

"What are you doing here? I said I'd phone if there was an update."

"I just wanted to check in on my nephews."

I rolled my eyes but didn't respond to that.

"No update?"

"The same as before. Colton could wake up at any second or…"

Dave sighed. He leaned his hands on the railing by the bed's foot. I wanted to tell him to step away from the bed. To just leave us alone. And it became clear that my anger was not directed solely at the four men kept in some dark room somewhere in the greater New Jersey area. A significant portion of it was directed at this man hovering over Colton's hospital bed right now.

"I need to talk to you about business."

I stood up slowly, stretching my legs. "I need to piss."

Dave winced at the crudeness but remained standing over Colton. "I'll wait."

When I was done relieving my bladder I walked back into the room, taking a moment to study Dave from behind. He was old. It seemed that Dave aged a decade overnight. His slumped shoulders gave him an air of defeat. His hanging head made him seem like a loser. Why had I ever been afraid of him?

"I'm not discussing business with Colton fighting for his life. Make the decisions that you think need to be made. I don't want to know anything right now."

Dave turned around and I stood my ground. Despite his defeated posture, his eyes were still as fiery as ever. "Are you mad at me?"

"Colton never wanted this life. Neither did I, come to think of it. But I did things that I have to take responsibility for, even though they were thrust upon me. Colton never did anything to deserve any of this."

There was the faintest twitch in the corner of Dave's mouth, something that any other person wouldn't even have picked up. But I did.

"Look at you," I said. "Your distaste for Colton is so evident you can't even hide it. Notice, Uncle Dave, that I didn't say hatred. Which is what Colton always thought you had for him. But it's not hatred, it's something much worse. It's indifference. You don't care about him at all, do you? Whether he lives, whether he dies. Doesn't matter one way or the other."

"That's a lie!"

"Fuck you. The only reason you pretend to give a damn is because of me. And not because you love me. Let's be honest. I'm your vanity project. I'm the one who is to keep your legacy alive, am I right, *Uncle* Dave? But more importantly, I'm the cash cow for this family. I keep everyone rolling in it. Well, I'm not signing another damn document or doing anything else until you finally admit to it."

Dave ran a heavy hand through the little bit of hair he had left. "Admit what, Jason?" he asked tiredly.

"That you never really cared about us. Not the way you pretended you did."

"That's ridiculous."

"I don't care either way. I'll tell you now. Once Colton is back on his feet and I've sorted this mess with Grey and the others, we're done. I'm cashing our chips in and we're out of this life that you fucking dumped on us."

"Who says he'll ever wake up again?" Dave asked softly.

The question was barely introduced to the universe before a soft groan emanated from behind Dave, and I rushed to the bed.

My face would be the first one Colton got to see when he woke up.

When I stood next to Colton, his eyes were looking up at me but it seemed like he didn't know who I was. The look on his face wasn't one of happiness, it was one of confusion.

"I'll go inform them," Dave said and stepped out of the room.

I grabbed Colton's hand and held it. "Colton," I said softly and tears streamed through my eyes uncontrollably, no matter how much I tried to stop them. I felt a weak squeeze from Colton's side but still no recognition in his eyes.

The hospital staff barged in and took over, and I had to stand aside like a fucking spectator, unable to do anything but wait. They started doing their checks and finally took him off the ventilator. That was a good sign, right? I had to believe that it was. The doctors said some stuff to Colton, but he never actually responded. *I'm afraid I don't have any good news except for the fact that your brother's going to be alive.*

But I didn't care. Whatever happened, whatever brain damage he had suffered, we could find a way to keep him alive. Right now, I wanted Colton alive, even if he was in a wheelchair for the rest of his life. I started biting my nails, something I hadn't done in years. The worst part was I didn't know I was doing it until I had already bitten off a substantial portion of dead skin. The two doctors in the room were exchanging looks, and I had no idea what that meant. They wouldn't say a word. *That can't be good.* Fucking stop with the drama already you idiots! Didn't they realize what I was going through? That I needed answers!

"So um," I finally managed to compose myself long enough to ask. I realized how afraid I was of asking that question. Because once the question was out there, they would need to respond to it, and I wasn't sure if I was ready to hear whatever came after that. *Get a hold of yourself you moron.* "How is he?"

One of the doctors, who was flashing a tiny light in Colton's eyes, stood up straight and looped the stethoscope around his neck. "Mr. Hamilton," he said, and I still couldn't decipher what was on his face. "Your brother seems fine."

But he was just looking at me with that odd look in his eyes. "Doctor, when he saw me, I don't think he recognized me."

"Oh, that's quite normal," the doctor said. "His brain went through a lot in the past few days. It's normal to be a little disoriented for a while. Not to forget he's on heavy medication."

"So, he's fine?" I almost couldn't believe it. It sounded too good to be true.

The doctor came towards me and placed a hand on my shoulder, even gave me a smile so I could see that everything was truly okay. "He has a long way to go before you can say he's fine," said the doctor. "But there's no brain damage. With a bit of rehab and the right amount of medication, he'll be well on his way to recovery in no time."

He's right. But still, this had to be the hard part, right? I cautiously made my way towards Colton who was already asleep. Before I could ask, the doctor explained it to me. "He's heavily medicated. The drugs should wear off in a day or two. Until then, he might be disoriented and he may be unable to talk much. He might not even be awake most of the time. But we assure you, Mr. Hamilton, none of this is cause for concern."

Everything was cause for concern. But they were doctors. They didn't understand. They only viewed my brother as a patient and, to them, he may have looked okay. But I knew that wasn't true. No matter what I tried to tell myself, I knew the worst wasn't over. That time hadn't even arrived yet. I saw what they did to him. I had all those videos, recording every bit of torture they had put him through. I had seen them bring him to the brink of death. I was the one of who had pulled him out and if I had been late, fuck, I can't even go there. But in so many ways I was already late. The doctors and nurses left the room and that gave me a chance to allow myself to break. I could finally be weak, shed tears. I sat next to Colton and watched him. Just looking at him *hurt*. I felt a very real pang of sudden aching in my chest. The bastards who did this would get what's coming to them. *You were late, Jason. You let this happen. You shouldn't even be able to see yourself in the mirror.* My conscience was right. I messed up. I should have left when Colton suggested it. I should have just done what I wanted to do, what I knew was right for us instead of fucking doing my uncle's bidding.

I'm sorry, Colton.

But being sorry doesn't change anything I know. I will allow myself this moment of weakness, but then I will get back on my feet and go back to what's really important. Revenge. Showing those people the gravity of what they had done. I felt a hand on my shoulder. "Dave—" I was about to tell him to fuck off when I noticed that it wasn't Dave who had entered the room without my knowledge. "Gary?"

"I'm sorry, sir. Hope I'm not interrupting."

"It's okay."

"How's he doing? What do the doctors say?"

"They say he's out of the woods."

"Well, that's good."

"Yeah."

There was a pause as I waited for Gary to come out with what he had really come here to say. "There's some news," he said at last, "that I thought you should hear right away, sir. It's about Devyn."

My ears pricked as I tried to maintain a calm façade. "Did he try to break out again?"

"No sir," Gary explained. "This is actually some intel on his family that you requested."

"What is it, Gary? What's the intel?"

Gary handed me a manila envelope. "Perhaps it would be better if you could see for yourself, sir."

4
JASON

The last face I wanted to see in intensive care was that of Detective Paulson.

A bunch of other officials walked inside the room along with him, and all I could do was clench my fists, hoping that the anger wouldn't show. Paulson looked smug, like he knew something I didn't, and I hated when people looked at me that way.

"Detective," I said, almost joyously. "Didn't expect to see you here so soon. My brother hasn't even been awake a few hours."

Even though officially Colton had come out of the coma two days ago, it was only today that he looked awake. He started speaking a few words here and there, and when I came in a few minutes back, he actually said more than a sentence. So to see the detective here so soon seemed a little odd. But Paulson didn't look bothered one bit. "I'm aware of that, Mr. Hamilton," he said. "I'm here to take his statement before anyone threatens him into saying something they want him to say, instead of what really happened."

It was obvious the statement was directed toward me. But I didn't let that faze me. In all the excitement of seeing Colton open his eyes and those tubes being taken out, I'd forgotten the reality of it for a moment. It was my mistake and I would have to deal with the consequences. Colton had barely spoken, but the doctors said that was normal for someone in his condition.

"The doctors said not to give him undue stress." I tried to stall.

"Don't worry, Mr. Hamilton," Paulson said, handing me a document. "The doctor himself approved this visit." I had no need to look at the document to see if Paulson was telling the truth. I quietly watched him click his pen as he turned to Colton.

"So, Colton," Paulson began. "I'm sorry I have to talk about all this when you're clearly going through something horrible but that's the job, I'm afraid."

"It's okay," Colton said. I could see on his face how uncomfortable he was now that the detective had entered the room. But like me, he probably realized that the only way out of this was through this, so he kept the conversation going.

"Son, what they did to you," Paulson said. "It's appalling. And they should be punished for it, every single one of them, don't you think?"

"I guess."

"But you realize… vigilante justice is illegal and carries consequences. You don't want that. Let the law and the justice system do their job. They might be bastards, son but there are certain rights a human being enjoys in this world. Those rights, this civilization, are what keeps us human. If everyone were to take revenge on every person who harmed them, this world would be in chaos."

I couldn't help the chuckle that emanated from my throat.

Paulson turned to me. "Mr. Hamilton, is there something you would like to say?"

"You're joking, right?" I said. "Someone put a gun to my brother's head and tortured him for weeks, and you did nothing to stop it. Sounds to me like the world is already in chaos, Detective."

The Detective directed his next question to Colton. "Taking revenge is illegal, Colton. It could land you or whoever else in jail. Do you want to live the rest of your life in prison? Go back to being in some cell?"

Colton glanced at his feet. "No sir."

"Well, son," the Detective added, "then you need to talk to me."

"What would you like to know?"

Paulson tried again. "I don't want a lot from you. I know you're healing and you need time. But if those criminals get too far during that time, you'll never be able to forgive yourself."

Colton gave a nod.

"People like that shouldn't be out in the open or they could hurt someone else. You don't want anyone else to go through this, do you?" the Detective said.

Colton looked uncomfortable again.

"Don't let them guilt you into saying anything you don't want to," I said to Colton.

"Jason," Paulson interrupted me. "I'm the one doing the questioning here and I'm the one carrying the badge. I could have you kicked out of this room if I wanted."

I knew that wasn't true and I'm sure so did the Detective. But he was playing a game as always, trying to have the upper hand. So far, I was doing fine, but everything now depended on Colton's response and that scared me.

"So," Paulson directed his attention back to Colton. "Come on, son. Do you know who those people were? A name? Moniker? Tattoos? Do you remember anything?"

Colton's eyes were wet. *Colton, please don't do it.* I said a little prayer and crossed my fingers. I refused to look Paulson in the eye. Colton was looking right at me and I smiled, simply to look like I had nothing to hide.

"No," Colton said. His voice was low; he was having trouble speaking the words due to the hurt jaw, but the word was clearly enunciated.

Paulson looked like he might be in shock. His eyes widened and then narrowed, and I saw his Adams apple throb as he swallowed. But on the surface, he kept a calm profile. "You're saying," he began, "you don't remember *anything*?"

Colton stopped looking at me and his eyes fell to his legs on the hospital bed. His head leaned forward. He had a dejected look on his face. I knew he was hiding his tears but Paulson didn't know that. "I don't remember."

Paulson took a while in coming to his next question but it was obvious he was disappointed. "Do you at least remember who broke you out?" Paulson was looking right at me when he asked that question. *Look at me all you want pal, this isn't in your hands.* And then Colton looked at me too. His eyes were still filled with tears. It was my turn to waver my gaze around everything at the room except for Colton and the Detective. I rubbed my neck, hoping for this moment to be over before I blew a blood vessel inside my head.

Colton's response was more forceful this time, unwavering. "No."

"No?" Paulson said, trying to be calm but he was having a tough time doing it. "What do you remember?"

"I remember a bunch of guys torturing me to no end!" Colton snapped. "Isn't that enough?"

Those were the first lengthy phrases my brother had spoken in a long time. Paulson realized it was futile and angrily clicked his pen shut. He shoved his little notebook inside his jacket pocket and took out a business card. He handed it to my brother. "Why don't you hang on to this?" he offered. "In case you think of something. That's my direct line."

Colton palmed the card but didn't bother to read what was on it. He started fidgeting with it. Paulson saw this and smiled. "I know you see this uniform and you think *fucking cop bastard, what does he know*?" Paulson placed a light kiss on Colton's bandaged head. "I know this uniform is tainted. I know you've probably lost faith in it because you've seen your brother and your uncle make these uniforms dance, like fucking marionettes. But I'm not one of them. This uniform isn't tainted, Colton, because I'm not tainted. Your brother hates me because he can't control me. I'm a threat to his 'business.' He has no choice, Colton, but you do. You have a choice to come clean and walk out unscathed from all of this. You're the victim now, but if your family ends up turning you into the same shit that they are, then there will be no going back. Then even I won't be able to help you."

Paulson left the room and I went over to Colton who was still staring at the business card. "You didn't tell them the truth. Why?"

"I saw your face. I knew you wanted me to keep it a secret."

"If you had told them who brought you back, or even if you'd told Paulson any of their names, everything would have been ruined."

"Everything is already ruined."

The words bore through my chest.

I took the card from him and tossed it in the trashcan next to the hospital bed. Maybe that act gave me some form of control, or maybe I was just mad at Paulson for putting that stuff in my brother's head. Colton stayed silent and didn't say a word.

"He's a cop, Colton. They're trained to mess with your head. You don't actually believe the crap he just told you, do you?"

"I'm tired."

Was Colton hiding something from me? Had Paulson's words actually made an impact on him and he wasn't telling me? I had no way of finding out, but I was going to make sure that the Detective didn't come by anymore. The less Colton saw of him the better. I helped Colton settle into a more comfortable position on the bed and adjusted the pillows. "Is that better?"

He gave a tiny nod to indicate *yes*.

"I'm going to be right here, okay?"

"Why don't you go home?" Colton said. "Dave said you haven't had much sleep."

"I'm fine."

"Jason. Do it for me?"

I guess my brain was kind of fried to be honest. A bit of rest couldn't hurt. But I hated leaving my brother alone. Of course, the doctors did say he was out of danger now.

"I'm just going to be asleep anyway," Colton urged. "I don't want you to sleep here, it's torture. So please. Go home. Rest. Come back when you're feeling better. I'm not going anywhere."

I knew that all this was true, that there was no way anyone could get a hold of him with all the security and the nursing staff, but I still couldn't bring myself to feel at peace about it.

"Okay," I leaned in to kiss his cheek. "I'll see you soon."

Colton said nothing.

He turned his back to me and slept.

5

JASON

I had prepared myself. And so had Colton's doctor and the counselor I relented to speak to for two minutes at everyone's insistence. But it still stung. How could it not? The person who had woken up from that coma wasn't my brother. Or it was, but it wasn't. When I looked into his eyes, it was the same eyes I remembered, but it wasn't Colton. Those eyes weren't filled with laughter and mischief and life. They were glassy and dead.

But as I helped Colton up in the bed and adjusted the pillows behind him, I relented and sank my face into his hair and inhaled him. It was at that moment, as the scent of my brother filled me, that determination rose like a tsunami inside me. I was going to pull him through this, even if I had to drag him by the balls of his feet. I was going to be the one to pull him out of this darkness, to reach inside his head where he was hiding and bring him back to the land of the living.

I'd been there in time. I had saved him. He hadn't died in some filthy pit in the forest. So I was not going to let him drown now. I kissed Colton's head before pulling away, but he didn't react. If anything, the intimate gesture we had shared countless times before left him looking uncomfortable. I ran my hand through my hair and settled back in my chair opposite Colton's bed and ran through emails on my phone while he fed himself, giving him space.

It killed me not having my mouthy little brother with me in the room. All I wanted was for him to talk my ears off about some stupid thing of the moment he was obsessed about. That, and I wanted to take the spoon from his shaky hand and feed him the porridge that he spent twenty minutes dealing with. But he'd freaked out when I offered to do it before, so I refrained from doing it again.

"I bet you're going crazy for a cheeseburger right now."

Colton didn't react, and I wasn't even sure he'd heard me. But after a moment the spoon clattered against the plastic bowl and he turned to me. Those eyes that were devoid of the emotions I needed to see stared at me for a moment, and it left me disconcerted. But then Colton finally spoke to me. I wished now the silence had continued.

I watched as he flipped the plastic bowl of porridge over and it ran all over his blanket. "I'm not going crazy for a cheeseburger. I'm going crazy *inside*! I don't want to eat this fucking slop! But I'm doing it for you! I don't want to breathe. I wish I'd died out there. In fact, I'm sure I did. I'm exhausted. *I don't have it in me to make you feel better right now!*"

I stood and tried to calm him down, but Colton started ripping the IVs from his skin and throwing the vases and flower arrangements and bottles of medication at his bedside drawer.

"Colton, calm down…"

"I'm sorry I'm not happy to be alive! I'm sorry I'm not grateful I get to deal with the memories in my head for the rest of my life!" As I held my brother down while he thrashed and tore open his stitches and bumped his head wound bloody against the headboard, I was equal parts thankful for him finally showing some emotion and dying inside with him.

"Calm down, Colton! Please!"

"*Fuck you!*" he bawled. "Why should I trust you, you're just like everyone else!"

The nurse injected something into the drip to knock Colton out, and he finally succumbed into an uneasy sleep. I looked so pathetic standing over my brother, crying, that the hardline bitch even took pity on me and offered to give me something for my anxiety, too.

"I don't deserve peace," was all I said to her undeserved, kind gesture, and she left me standing vigil over my broken baby brother.

"I don't know how," I whispered to Colton, "but I'll make this right."

****

"You shouldn't be here."

"My nephew's getting out of hospital, I should be here," Dave said piously.

"Gary's here," I argued. "He'll get us home. There's no need for you to hang around and upset Colton."

"Jason, I'm here. Deal with it."

I was in the mood to argue. Dave's condescending posturing was just the thing that threatened to send me over the edge. But as I stared at Colton's room and waited for him to finish getting dressed, I reminded myself this was not about me. So I slowed my breathing and folded my arms, hating Dave even more for making me feel like a child again.

"How is he doing?"

"The fuck do you care?"

"For God's sake, Jason, I'm here aren't I?"

I was about to retort when Gary stepped up out of nowhere and hunched over Dave, giving him the update. I didn't give a damn about them or anything else when Colton's door opened and he stood leaning against the frame, looking totally exhausted. I was at his side in a second.

"Here, sit down." I helped him into the wheelchair slowly. "I wish you'd let me help you get dressed." I was still smarting from Colton not letting me help him get changed. It was like he was shy around me now, for the first time in years. We'd seen each other in our birthday suits more times than I can recall, so I didn't get it. I kept telling myself it was only because he didn't want me to see all the bruises still mapping his body, instead of the alternative.

"I can dress myself," he said softly. At least he was talking to me more these days.

"There he is!" Dave stepped up to us, the picture of the caring uncle. He hunched down in front of Colton, fixing him with a long stare. "Are you excited to go back home today?"

"What are you doing here?" Colton said after a long pause.

I had to keep myself from laughing as Colton lifted his head and stared beyond Dave's shoulder, blanking him out. I took that as my cue and started wheeling the chair past Dave, leaving him hunched over on the floor staring after us. He caught up just as we stepped through the elevator Gary was holding open for us.

"I'll wait until you're all settled in and then we can have dinner, the whole family."

Dave was fraying my nerves, but Colton just sat staring at the doors before him as we descended the floors. If he didn't have the energy to make me feel better, I was sure he wouldn't exhaust himself on Dave's account. We exited the lift and left the hospital, both

Colton and I breathing easier for the first time in a very long time.

6
COLTON

I stared at the bed.

All those memories, the good ones, the ones related to Jason.

But somehow it felt as though they had been tarnished.

It was my room, well, *our* room, but I felt like a stranger.

"Colton?"

"Yeah?"

"Will you put this on?"

I turned my attention from the bed to Jason who was holding a ring. I noticed there was one on Jason's finger. "You found them," I said, and the memory of hiding those rings in the medicine cabinet seemed to be from a different life.

He showed me his ring. "We're together," he said. "Forever, Colton."

"I uh… I got these before you told me you were proposing to that girl… Uncle Dave…"

"Colton, I was never going to propose to her," Jason said, coming toward me. "I let you think that the last time we were together because I wanted to surprise you when you came back on your next break. I was going to ask you to be with me."

That should have made me happy.

But I wasn't sure I could ever feel happiness of any kind. Ever. "When I was… you know… there… Jason, they showed me something. A video. You. With some girl… Jason, I'm not complaining, just… "

Jason looked a bit taken aback. "Was it in the alley of the club?"

"Yeah."

"And the girl. She was in a blue dress?"

"I guess."

"Those fucks."

"Jason, you don't have to—"

"I was at the bar, getting drunk because well, because I was fucked up! And this girl offers me a drink, says she wants to just sit there and drink with me. So I said what the hell. And then I don't remember much… but I was drunk so I blamed it on the booze, but I still remember her words… she told me not to drink too much because it was easy to drug me or something… I don't remember exactly but she said she drugged me. I remember getting a blowjob but not much else… and I couldn't understand then… why anyone would do that but I do now!"

I didn't know what to say to that so I kept quiet.

Jason took that as a sign that I was angry. "Fuck, Colton you have every right to be mad," he said. "But you don't think I'd fuck someone while you were in hell, do you?"

I knew he was telling the truth. "No."

Jason held my hands. "I don't ever want us taking these rings off."

"Jason—"

"I mean it, Colton. And if you ever see this ring off my finger, know that something truly awful has happened."

Jason tried to kiss me and I started to have a panic attack. The whole world started to spin…

"Colton, what's wrong?"

"I… I… uh… need to lie down…"

"It must be the meds," Jason was saying. "The doctors said they were going to make you dizzy, but you need to take them for a while."

Jason helped me get on the bed, and I could barely stand the touching but I had no choice. I couldn't even see through the fog in front of my eyes. The attack got better the minute I was in bed. Everything seemed to have calmed down a little. I was able to breathe and the dizziness, although still there, wasn't that bad anymore. Jason was taking off my shoes and he tossed them aside. He was about to unbutton my jeans when my hand almost moved of its own volition and stopped his from going any further. "No!" I protested without wanting to.

Jason stopped. "Colton, it's just…"

"Please," I said. "Leave them on. I'm fine."

"Okay," Jason left it at that thankfully, and I felt embarrassed but unable to get past it. What the hell was I doing? This was Jason. Not them. I knew he wasn't going to hurt me. So why was I reacting this way? I wanted to scream.

Jason stood next to me. "Do you want me to stay here or leave?"

Oh God. Why was he asking? "Jason… I…"

"Say no more," Jason said. "I'll be in the other room, okay? I don't think I'll get much sleep so just tell me if you need anything."

"I'm sorry."

"Don't be sorry," Jason said and kissed my forehead. "Are you going to be okay?"

I don't think I was ever going to be okay but I nodded.

"Okay then. I'll see you in the morning, Colton."

With that he was gone.

I turned to my side, watching the curtains that came in view. It felt strange being on this bed. So comfortable. In a place that was my own. I could do anything, go anywhere, even if I was just going to lie down because the doctor said I needed to let my body heal, I was still *free*. I had to pinch myself several times, to actually come to terms with the fact that I had freedom, that I wasn't handcuffed to some tiny cot anymore or confined to a depressing hospital bed, that I had a nice bed to lie on and this house had everything that could provide me comfort, including Jason.

I closed my eyes and tried to feel that peace.

The ring stayed on my finger, feeling a little strange but fitting perfectly.

7
JASON

I lay on the bed in the guestroom but sleep was miles away from me.

How could I sleep when my brother was in that kind of pain? When I could see everything that they did to him right in front of me? Colton's body was a roadmap of scars, each one chronicling a moment of terror he'd had to live through. What disturbed me most was how much it got to me.

I was no stranger to torture. Looking away and pretending like life was fair and peaceful had always been a luxury no one in my lifestyle could afford. So I shouldn't have been so shocked when I caught a glimpse of Colton's exposed torso. But the crisscross of jagged scars dancing across his abdomen punched me hard in the gut. Harder than I was willing to admit.

Perhaps it was the thought of him suffering through each of those blows. That I saw the moment each of those scars were inflicted on him when I looked in his eyes. Fuck. How did he even function, much less find the will to get out of bed?

I closed my eyes in the dark of the room hoping to block out the images of the yellowing, healing bruises that had caught my eye. But the fireworks behind my eyelids just taunted me, dancing in front of me like little-jagged knives sticking into the black figure around it, into Colton, and I couldn't do anything to stop it.

I yelled past the lump in my throat and sat up, greasy from a heavy sweat. I wiped my face and looked for the red alarm clock. It was 3:15AM. I'd only been able to get two hours' sleep, but I knew it would be pointless chasing it anymore so I kicked the covers off and got up. After I checked on Colton, who was breathing steadily and passed out under a haze of painkillers, I stripped down and walked to the master bathroom.

Running the shower cold, I stepped under the bruising torrent of uncomfortable water and let it pelt against my skin, reminding me that I was alive. I was fucked up and it scared me. I wasn't scared for me. I was afraid for Colton. If I was not at the top of my game, what chance did he have? I was his only real ally. I was his only hope of getting his life back. Me falling apart was an indulgence neither of us could afford.

There would be no falling apart, from either of us. I didn't care if Colton would kick me in the gut in the morning, or call me every name under the sun, but I was going to drag him to the land of the living. My brother was still in there somewhere. He was still there and as long as Colton was there, I wouldn't give up on him. Just like I knew he wouldn't have given up on me had the tables been reversed.

That thought sent a shiver up my spine that had nothing to do with the cold water I was toweling off my body. I hung my head in shame, ashamed of my weakness at the thought of suffering through what he had. I leaned against the en suite's door and stared at Colton's sleeping frame. Everyone had always assumed I was the strong one. That wasn't the case at all, as Colton had now finally proved to the world.

*****

"What's this?"

"Food." I bit into a charred piece of bacon. "Eat it."

Colton pushed his plate away, getting grease on the bed. "You should've asked me before you went to the trouble."

"Yeah, and you would've said you're not hungry. Which is why I didn't."

"Which is why you should've."

I bit into another piece of bacon and stared Colton down. "I said eat your food." I eyed him a bit longer, not backing down, when Colton finally pulled the plate closer to him.

I was relieved to have won that battle, but I was sure I would. Despite everything, Colton still listened to me. He picked up an equally charred piece of bacon and chewed on it obnoxiously, crunching his way through his breakfast and making me smile.

"Good?"

"Tastes like horse shit."

"Watch it," I warned him, my smile vanishing.

Colton ignored me and piled scrambled egg on his toast. Apparently his appetite was returning.

"Talking about horses," I said, executing the next stage of my hostile takeover of his day. "Obviously we can't go riding yet, but I thought we could go for a hike down at the ranch. Pet the horses before going for a picnic by the river."

"Picnic? Since when do you go on picnics?"

I refused to rise to the bait, and shoved fried mushrooms in my mouth. After swallowing, I continued. "I want you to get out into the sun, into open space. The doctor says you need exercise, so a walk at the ranch will do you good."

"I'm tired."

"We're going."

"My back hurts."

"We're going."

"Fuck you."

"You too. We're going!"

Colton crossed his arms across his chest and stared at me from under a bush of eyebrows. I crossed my arms and stared back at him. His shoulders were the first to sag.

That was the end of that.

8
COLTON

It had been too long since we visited the ranch. I'd always been on Jason's case to get him to take me, but he'd always humored me and told me to go on my own, he'd go with me the next time. Now it was him bringing us down there and the irony wasn't lost on me.

Walking behind Jason was a challenge. The burns on the soles of my feet still stung like a mother, but I wasn't about to let him know that. I knew what he was doing, though. He was as well aware of my stubbornness as I was of his. He was challenging me, pushing me out of my comfort zone. Walking just a bit too fast for me to stay comfortably with him. So that I had to push myself just that little bit more.

Walking up to River, I was happy in that moment to be where I was. Twenty minutes earlier I would've been happy to spend the whole day on my back in the bed watching cable TV. Now, seeing my beautiful steed and running my hands through his soft mane, I was thankful to Jason for pulling me out of that slump.

Not that I would tell him that, of course.

I closed my eyes and pushed my face into the soft hair and inhaled slowly. It was a clean scent, a warm smell of River that filled me, and with it brought memories of days spent riding with Jason and my other friends. I'd been so proud of Jason's equestrian skills, my chest physically swelled when he did some amazing trick that got all my friends gasping for breath and yelling at me what a cool older brother I had. I wanted to tell them I already knew as I watched him sweep over rocky terrain looking like a young warrior on his way to battle, gracious and beautiful and manly.

"What are you thinking about?"

I pulled my face away from River and opened my eyes. Jason's eyes were so unguarded, so sincere that I couldn't get my guard up in time before blurting, "Indiana Jones."

That was all he needed, as it all fell into place for both of us. I'd always called him my Indiana Jones when we rode around alone, and he'd act like it annoyed him, but I saw him sit up a little bit straighter on his horse every time I called him that.

"Ready for a walk?"

I shifted uncomfortably on my feet, gauging my pain level. Luckily, Jason threw me a lifeline.

"Hey, let's take the buggy down to the river. Maybe we can walk around there after putting our feet in the stream for a while?"

I smiled, far from put off by the idea. I enjoyed the openness of the buggy, the wind in my face and the sun roasting my head as we drove down to the river in silence. I had completely given up on seeing the sun ever again not so long ago. The thought of taking a picnic under a shaded tree with rolled up pants and my feet in a cold stream with Jason sitting next to me was a dream I hadn't even dared to consider. And here we are.

After throwing rocks into the water and trying to make them skip from where we were seated, I stretched my back lazily.

"I don't know about you but I'm starving," Jason said after a while.

"I don't know about you, but I'm not getting up to fetch the food," I said, keeping my eyes on the clean water making its way down the stream.

"Figures," Jason muttered under his breath and got up as I smiled smugly.

Placing the basket between us like a prize trophy, Jason flopped back down in the spot he'd recently vacated and scoured the ground for more rocks to throw into the river.

I delved into the basket, expecting to find berries, cheese, crackers and wine. My fingers grazed against wax sandwich wrap and I delved deeper, pulling out a wrapped little missile from the basket. I stared at Jason wordlessly as realization dawned.

"You didn't?"

Jason smiled his goofy grin where he was secretly proud of himself, but acted like he wasn't bothered. "You thought I'd gotten some generic picnic basket from the market, didn't you?"

I didn't say anything. Instead, I unwrapped the hot dog only to find a fresh bun with a hot dog in the middle slathered with mustard and ketchup. It was a simple combination, but one that Jason and I both loved. My mom had shucked tradition of always trying to outdo everyone else on picnics, and this was her go-to menu for us.

We grew up on ketchup and mustard hot dogs at picnics, and soda and potato barbecue potato crisps. That was it, and that was all we wanted. It was the best picnic menu either of us could wish for, and the fact that Jason went out of his way to do this for me choked me up.

I didn't know what to say to him, so I stuffed my face with hot dog while he poured soda and opened the potato chips.

"I hope you didn't just make a couple of dogs," I said eventually when I licked my fingers clean of spilled ketchup and mustard goo. I could do with another half a dozen probably.

"What do you think?" Jason asked and scooped a streak of mustard off my shirt and licked his finger slowly. "Can't take you anywhere."

I smiled at him, really smiled for the first time since I'd been back, and his surprise at it broke my heart all over again.

*****

"I admit nothing."

"Oh please," Jason said. "You had a good time. I know it. So don't pretend you were anything but *enthralled*."

"Whatever," I said. Standing by the massive window of our room, I could see the backyard pool and a hot-looking Latino pool boy carrying a big net. He had to be a new hire. I'd never seen him before. Jason paid a woman named Stephanie to hire people on his behalf and look after the house in general. I wanted to give her a standing ovation for picking this particular guy. His body was tanned from working in the sun, and there were barely a few inches of skin visible underneath the ink. He was muscled, and my gaze kept going from his six-pack abs to the bulge inside his blue bathing suit. I could smell the sweat on his skin and the chlorine from where I was standing. As he moved the skimmer along the pool's surface, the muscles in his tanned arms swelled and contracted. The sun was warm that day despite the approaching fall and I almost wanted to take a dip myself.

"Like what you see, baby brother?" I felt Jason's arm tightening around my waist and pulling me toward him. I could feel the hardness in his white shorts. He nuzzled my neck and I let my head fall back on his shoulder.

Jason grabbed my crotch and tugged. "Maybe there's something in here that needs cleaning?"

I almost laughed. "He's a pool boy," I said, letting Jason touch me through the shorts. "Unless you're hiding a fifteen-foot water body up your ass, I don't see a reason why he'd be in here."

"You let me worry about that," Jason said, tenderly kissing my neck. "Just tell me if you need him to clean or not."

I turned to face Jason, his arms still around me. "You're telling me you can get that six-foot tall drink of straight to clean *our* pool?"

"Say the magic words," Jason's nose grazed mine.

I knew I should have been thinking about what was happening here but for one, I was certain Jason was going to come back a loser and I would love to hold that over his head for as long as we lived, and the other thing was this strange need I felt inside to see how things would turn out. "Yes."

Jason grinned. "I'll be back," he said, and winked. When he left the room, I turned back to the pool boy who was now lying flat on his back to rest or to take in more sun perhaps. All I know is that watching him was *torture*. And then, I saw Jason approach him and I was surprised to realize how much I wanted Jason to actually come back a winner. Jason took him aside and then they were out of my field of vision. I drummed my fingers on the windowsill, trying to stay calm but inside I was a mess and couldn't stay still.

The door opened and Jason stepped inside. "Come on in," he said to someone standing outside and I turned, stuck my hands inside the pockets of my shorts to keep from fidgeting. The pool boy walked in, wearing the same bathing suit and nothing more.

Jason introduced us. "Colton, meet Emilio."

I don't know why I was sweating so hard. "Hi."

Emilio walked in and Jason closed the door and locked it. "You're... *brothers*."

"Is that a problem?" Jason asked, coming toward me and putting his arms around me, kissing my neck.

"If it's not a problem for you, why should I care?" Emilio replied and walked a few steps closer. "Look, I'll be straight. Nothing too kinky. The whole incest thing is as far as it gets. Also, I don't get fucked up the ass. We can do just about anything else."

"Let me guess," Jason said. "Not your first rodeo—in this case not-so-straight orgy."

"Well, technically it's a three-way. And yes. Let's just say I've had a few interesting experiences."

"Fine. We'll work around your 'rules' so you can keep pretending you're still straight. Right, Colton?"

I wanted to reply but couldn't think of words to actually say something. Jason walked up to stand in front of me and grabbed my crotch, ran a firm hand up and down it while he kissed me. I placed my hand behind his head and pulled him closer. His hand traveled inside my shorts and he squeezed and fondled me, until I was hard. Then he dropped to his knees, pulled down my shorts and I felt his mouth on my cock. A few moans escaped my throat, and it felt odd, doing it in front of some stranger. I opened my eyes. The way Emilio was looking at me, I knew he was far from being straight. He was running a hand over that bulge, and then he took out his cock, big and beautiful, just like him, and started tugging at his erection, while his eyes still gazed at the two of us. In between he gave me those stares, unabashedly gazing into my eyes, and I don't know if he was doing it for my benefit or trying to make it look more exciting. Of course, the way he handled that cock, as he looked at us, it definitely wasn't his first time. As he came closer, he kissed me. When he broke off, we were looking at each other.

Jason stood and kissed me again. "He's beautiful, isn't he?"

"I won't lie," Emilio said. "I've fantasized about being with both of you. I just didn't think it would be at the same time."

"Well then," Jason lifted Emilio's arm and placed it on my cock. "This is your lucky day."

Emilio took the cue and started stroking me. He leaned in and kissed me. I thought Jason might have a problem with it, but he seemed strangely okay with everything. I felt a twinge of disappointment and tried to get over it by getting more into pool boy's kiss. I reminded myself how hot he was, how much he seemed to want me. *Even if Jason didn't.* I tried to push that thought out of my mind by whispering in Emilio's ear. "I want you to fuck me." If Jason could do it, so could I. Pool-boy grabbed me and pushed me on the bed. He stood there, stroking himself and I watched.

"Colton wait," Jason interrupted. "Are you sure about this?"

"I'm sure," I replied and Emilio leaned in and we kissed.

"Colton!"

"I said I'm sure!" I turned to pool-boy. "There are condoms in the drawer."

Emilio grinned and got up.

"Wait!" Jason bellowed.

"What's the matter, Jason?" I said, turning to him. "Are you feeling left out? You can have him after we're done."

He grimaced.

Emilio must have noticed the tension in the room, because he stood there looking at the two of us. "Okay, what's going on here?" he said. "I feel like I stepped in the middle of something."

"Everything's fine," I said. "My brother thinks he knows what I want but he doesn't know *shit*."

"What is that supposed to mean?" Jason walked up to us.

I glared at him. "I should have known," I said. "You say you love me, but the minute a hot pool guy enters the picture, you act like you've just been released from prison! Devyn was right. He might have showed me what you were doing behind my back for his own reasons, but he was right about you."

Jason fake-laughed. "Oh, I get it. The guy who kidnapped you and *tortured* you for *months* is suddenly better than me?"

I chuckled but I wished those tears hadn't formed in my eyes. "Yeah. That's it, Jason. You *get* me."

"I told you the truth about that video," Jason said. "Whether you believe it or not is entirely up to you. I'm not going to stand here and defend myself."

Emilio grabbed his swimwear and slid it on. "And that would be my cue to leave."

"No!" I yelled. "You can't leave, I'm not done with you!"

Emilio turned to Jason.

"What're you looking at him for?" I was angrier now. "He doesn't own me! I'm free to make my own decisions!"

"No, you're not." Jason reached inside his pocket for his wallet and took out some cash. He held it up for Emilio but Emilio refused. "We never did anything so I don't want that," he said. Then he looked at me. "Whatever this is, I think you two should hash it out without involving other people. Okay?"

"Who do you think you are?" I glared at him. "To tell us what to do with our problems."

"Colton, he's just trying to be nice," Jason interjected.

"So now *you're* the authority on niceness?"

Emilio smiled and shook his head. "I'll see you around," he said, walking up to the door. "That is, if you don't end up firing me first."

"No one's firing you," Jason said. "Just remember what I told you. Don't tell anyone."

With Emilio gone, there was suddenly this huge matter we had to face and neither of us was willing to take the first step. I stood and headed to the bathroom when Jason grabbed my arm and slammed me into a wall.

"Let me go!" I shoved at him and Jason stood there, a little stunned. "You think you can just push me around, and I'll let you treat me that way?"

"I never heard you complain before!"

"Well, you never brought a stranger into our bed before either!"

"I only did that because I thought it's what you wanted!"

"Don't lie," I said. "You wanted to fuck him."

"And you didn't?" Jason yelled. "*I want you to fuck me, Emilio!* That wasn't me, Colton, that was you! You're such a hypocrite!"

"I only did that because I was angry." The truth came spilling before I could do anything about it.

Jason calmed down a little. "Look, I'm sorry okay? We won't do it again."

"That's not it."

"Then what?"

"I know you don't find me attractive anymore," I said. "And I don't blame you. It's completely understandable, but I'd like you to be honest with me."

"What the *hell* are you talking about?"

"Come on, Jason. I've been out of rehab for weeks now and you didn't once initiate anything! We even sleep in separate beds!"

"Colton, fuck. You *told* me you wanted to sleep in separate beds!"

"I know. But that was before… I didn't…" I was starting to see how ridiculous and desperate I sounded. "Forget it. Okay? Just forget it."

"The only reason I haven't fucked you is because I didn't think you were ready!"

"I wasn't," I said, trying to push back tears. "I still don't know to tell you the truth. I don't know what I want."

Jason came up to me and hugged me and I let him. "Colton, if I wanted someone else, I would have someone else. Don't you get it?"

"I don't want you to do it because you feel sorry for me."

Jason pushed me back into the wall and started kissing me. "Does this feel like a pity kiss to you?"

I looked into his eyes and it was all there. The love, the kindness, the desire. I don't know why I had ever questioned it. The last thing I wanted was to be away from him so why did I keep pushing him away? The only reason I made it out of that hell was because I knew I had someone waiting for me. The only reason I never considered killing myself was because I knew what it would do to him. There had been times, during that abduction and after, where the darkness took over and all I wanted was freedom. But something Jason did or said would keep me going another minute, another hour, another day…

"What're you thinking?"

"Nothing," I lied.

"Talk to me."

I had the sudden urge to leave everything behind and let myself fall so he could catch me. He must have the seen the tears I was trying to hide because he pulled my head close to his chest and held me. "I can't pretend to know what you're going through," he said. "But I promise you the worst is over."

As much as I wanted to believe it, I felt like I'd lost the ability to be positive about most things. But Jason smelled nice. He smelled as he always did—like home. There was no other way to describe it. I lifted my head and Jason kissed me, one hand on my chest and then he seemed to take in my face. "Trust me."

So I did and kissed him back.

He lowered himself to his knees on the carpet and started unbuttoning my shorts. "Jason—"

But before I could protest Jason had my cock in his mouth and he was sucking on it. All I could do was give in and lean against the wall, running my hands over his head. Watching him, his eyes half-closed and his mouth on my erect shaft, his hand going over my balls…

He turned me around and pulled down my shorts, started rimming me, and things were no longer in my control…

I wanted him, no, *needed* him.

Everything would be okay if he reached inside me and touched my heart, the deepest recesses of my body and if he fucked me raw. My nerves were frayed, on edge, but the mounting pleasure was taking over now, creating a soothing layer over everything until nothing remained in the world but me and him, until everything was a blur.

I felt Jason's hot breath on my neck. "Let's move to the bed."

Saying that, he grabbed my hand and took me to our bed. He took off his shirt and tossed it aside, then climbed on the bed and propped himself on his elbows. I followed suit and tossed my shirt on the floor right next to his, then climbed onto the bed. I lay back on the bed and, still propped up on one arm, Jason ran his other hand all over my chest and belly. His eyes were gazing directly into mine.

For a long time, that's all we did.

Jason touched my face with his fingers. "I missed you."

I closed my eyes when he nuzzled my neck, kissed my shoulders and my chest. I lay there and absorbed his desire-filled kisses and his passionate caresses. I moaned out loud when he reached below my navel and kissed the tip of my cock. I lowered his shorts with my hands, until I could touch his ass and when I could do it, I pulled him into me and we kissed again. Jason started teasing me, pulling away every time I'd try to kiss him so I had to work hard at it but this made my cock that much harder. "Stop that!" I said, laughing. Jason grinned. "You're not getting it that easy," he said. "Tell me how much you want me."

"I'm not doing that."

Jason pulled away and I grabbed his arm and held him there. "No."

"I want to hear it," he said.

"I want you, okay?"

"Not just me," Jason said. "You want my cock and my balls-deep in your ass. Isn't that right?"

"Yes."

"Say it."

"I want your cock and you… balls-deep in my ass."

"You're such a slut," Jason grinned.

"Ugh, get off me!"

"I'm not going anywhere."

"Jason!"

His mouth descended on my navel, his tongue leaving moist traces on my belly. He kept going lower and I had no choice but to lay back and let him. He lowered my shorts completely off me, and my instincts were kicking in again, the ones that kept resurfacing at intervals, telling me I should stop, reminding me someone else had been here, where Jason was now. I pushed those thoughts away and tried to focus on Jason who was lowering his mouth on my cock and sucking me off. And then he looked at me while he stroked his own cock. I watched his hand, as it went from tip to shaft, then over the balls, making his dick look harder every time he finished with a stroke.

"Turn around," Jason said, and I complied because I needed more, just as much as he did. The pleasure was becoming a torture and I needed to get to the finish line. I needed to *finish*. I wanted to get to the culmination point of my desire. I don't think I'd ever been so horny before. My balls were ready to explode. My dick was rock hard, constantly leaking precum. So when he came on top of me as I lay on my stomach with my back to him, I felt some of those conflicting feelings again.

I felt Jason's finger, lubing up my hole with his spit, and then he used the same finger to pry about, and it felt good.

"Do you want me to stop?"

"No…" I barely managed.

"You're sure?"

"Yes."

I felt the tip of Jason's cock replacing that finger and I panicked. "Wait!"

"What is it?"

"Will you please use condoms?"

"Colton—"

"Can we not argue about this right now?"

Jason seemed to think about it for a moment and then I heard him reach into the drawer for condoms and lube. I shivered when I felt the cold lube but it warmed up as soon as Jason thrust those fingers into me again. "Does this hurt?"

"No."

Even though that was pretty much a go-ahead from my side, Jason was going slow. He barely touched the tip to my hole, and pushed slowly, gently, giving me time to get used to the feeling. He thrust a little further and this time it did hurt, so Jason placed a hand over mine and intertwined my fingers with his, kept pushing slowly. But I was panicking again. Jason must have noticed because he stopped and kissed my back. "It's just me," he said, and placed another kiss. "It's just me, Colton."

"Yeah…"

He pushed more and it was still hurting. But I still wanted it. I wanted him further, deeper, more intense, more passionate. I had to remind myself to breathe. "Do you want me to stop?"

"No," I said, this time with more confidence.

But when he actually thrust again and went deeper, everything was a mess. My head was sending out thoughts haphazardly and one by one, I saw them, Devyn, Logan, Grey and the other one… Ash… I saw them doing to me again what they had done to me so many times before. I was going through it yet again, seeing the whole thing in flashes. I wanted to run but I knew there was no running away from them… I was trapped forever in this nightmare.

"Colton, you need to relax," I heard Jason's voice but my eyes were squeezed shut. I heard that but didn't fully comprehend the meaning so I did nothing in response. Jason had stopped and he was trying to calm me down, kissing down my back and speaking in my ear. "You'll get hurt if you don't relax." And then I heard him yelling out my name. "Colton! Hey!" He kissed my cheek and smoothed down my hair. "Relax, okay? Just let go. Trust me."

I guess I was afraid to tell him what was going on, I didn't want him to think I was crazy. But that's what I was, right? Crazy? Bat-shit insane? My insanely hot brother who loved me was with me on this amazing bed in this beautiful room and all I could do was think of *them*?

Relax.

So I did. I willed the muscles in my body to become less tense.

Jason squeezed my hand and started thrusting again.

He was right.

It didn't hurt this time. Instead, I felt his cock reaching that spot inside me, and hitting it again and again until I was back in the moment. Suddenly, the fear was gone as well. I was back to feeling the same pleasure I had felt back when Jason had slammed me against the wall and started going down on me a while back. Everything that followed was unbelievable. All this time without having a single orgasm, I guess I had forgotten how good it felt. The same goes for being with Jason in that way. It was familiar and filled with nostalgia. But it was also raw and powerful. I actually felt dizzy.

But even better than that, was the fact that when it ended neither of us moved. We just lay there, wrapped up in each other. And when Jason started kissing me again not so long after that first fuck, I wasn't surprised to see that I was ready for him. We clawed and kissed some more, and grabbed at each other the rest of the night.

Always a little satisfied.

Always a little unfulfilled.

9

JASON

The bar was almost empty but there was one guy talking loudly to the bartender about random things and it was obvious the bartender wasn't even humoring him. I went to sit next to the drunk, and realized he was young. Colton's age, perhaps a little older. Then I noticed the empty shot glasses.

"Hi," the drunk said loudly and extended a hand for me to shake. "I'm Nate."

I took his hand. "Jason."

"I'm cutting you off man," the bartender said. "The bar's about to close. If you could please leave now, that would be great."

"Is this how you talk to regular customers?"

"If by regular customer," the bartender interjected, "you mean the guy who regularly comes to fuck up the atmosphere, then yeah."

"Fuck you!" Nate said, standing up. "I don't need you! I need your stupid fucking bar! You think you're the only place that serves alcohol?"

The guy could barely walk and stumbled, taking out the money he owed, so I had to help him. He smiled at me when I did. "Thanks, Jason. That's very sweet of you."

The bartender whispered to Jason. "If you can take him off my hands," he said, "you don't have to pay for a drink in this place. Ever."

"That's fine," I said. "I'll take care of him."

Saying that, I hauled Nate out of the bar.

We stood by the sidewalk, smoking.

"So, Jason?" Nate said. "What were you doing in a gay bar this late?"

"The same thing everyone does in a gay bar this late."

He laughed. "It's never enough, is it?"

"What do you mean?"

"I mean, you look like you might have a life at home. I'm guessing that wedding ring has been there for a while."

It was actually the first time I had realized I was even wearing it. "You have a good eye."

"A lifetime of trust issues will do that to you."

"Why did you develop trust issues in the first place?"

"Long, depressing story that I don't want to bore you with."

"You can tell me if you want."

Nate looked at me. "You're hot," he said. "I'm hot. Can we cut to the chase?"

This time it was my turn to laugh. "You're interesting, I'll give you that."

"And yet," he said, "you won't even remember me come morning."

"You don't know that."

"Look Jason," he said. "You look like a nice guy. The kind who wouldn't lie to my face. You know? I actually appreciate that so let's not pretend this is more than what it really is."

"And what is *this*?"

"A hookup, and believe it or not, I'm fine with that."

"Don't you ever want more?"

He scoffed. "You have more, don't you?" he said. "You're still here like every single person I know, waiting for a random hookup to bring you relief from whatever it is you're running away from."

"I'm not running away," I said. "I *never* run away from things."

"That ring," Nate said. "Is it a guy or a girl?"

"Guy."

"Let me guess. Young, hot looking thing, that you thought you were in love with, but now you've come to realize love isn't all it's cracked up to be?"

"I'm not discussing my personal life with you," I said, a little angrily.

"What happened?"

"Nothing happened!"

"Something must have," Nate said. "Everything was going fine, until… something happens that changes everything. So what happened with you?"

"He got into an accident," I said.

"Ah. No wonder. Come on, why don't we talk on the way to my apartment?"

"How far is your apartment?"

"A few blocks."

I nodded and we started to walk.

"I took care of my sick mother for four years," Nate explained. "She had cancer that wouldn't leave. Sick people, you know, they suck the life out of you."

"That's a harsh thing to say. Anyone can get sick!"

"Yeah, but if I got sick, I'd say the same about myself."

"I can take care of my husband, it doesn't bother me."

"Oh please," Nate said. "If it didn't you wouldn't be here."

"I told you this has nothing to do with him!"

"But you're wrong, Jason."

I stopped walking. "I'm starting to think this was a bad idea."

Nate walked up to me and placed his hands on my face, started kissing me. I had no choice but to kiss him back, and it made me feel like shit because I couldn't stop thinking about Colton.

"Still think it's a bad idea?"

"Look. I thought I could do this, but I can't."

Nate came closer to me and grabbed my crotch. "That's my apartment, right there. Let's go inside and discuss this." His breath whispered on my face. It mostly smelled of tequila but not in a bad way.

"Nate, I can't."

Nate dropped to his knees and started unbuttoning my jeans. I tried to stop him but that just made him more forceful. "Stop that! There's people watching!"

"Just let me do this," he said. "I'm sure I can convince you to stay."

"Fine, I'm convinced! Please, just get up before anyone sees us."

He was grinning and then he walked to his building and led me inside. The building itself was a bit nasty but that was nothing new in the downtown area. The apartment on the other hand, was lush and classy. Minimalistic and clean lines, very little furniture. Nate went straight to the coffee pot and poured us two cups. The coffee was stale and bitter but it did the job. I felt more alert and so did Nate after ingesting at least two more cups of that slop.

For a long time, we just talked. It was unusual but I found myself getting into the conversation. I realized he wasn't as dumb or as one-dimensional as he seemed back at the bar. But I guess he liked playing a caricature of himself and once in a while he would say something incredibly insane, just to throw me off. It wasn't working. The conversation moved from his various escapades this whole week, to his mother dying. I, on the other hand, offered some half-truths and some plain lies.

"So tell me what he's like? That guy of yours?"

"He's beautiful," I said. "Inside and out."

"You really love him."

"I do."

"So what're you doing, Jason?"

"What do you mean?"

"I mean, why are you fucking it up?"

"I'm not fucking anything up," I said. "I told you. My being here is no reflection on us. It's merely a reflection on me."

"You're young," Nate said. "You should be out there looking, not settling down. I still feel like you're making a mistake, getting into a serious relationship so soon."

"You have to commit to something in life," I said. "Whether it's committing to being single or committing to being married. Committing to be in love or committing never to fall in love. And if you find someone that you even remotely think you can have a life with, you should take the risk. It's better than regretting something for the rest of your life and wondering what might have been. That's no way to live."

"When did you know you were going to commit to this guy?"

"I think I was always committed to him. We grew up together, so this wasn't something that happened randomly. We were always together. It wasn't hard."

Nate looked like he was about to burst into tears. But he kept his composure. "Have you ever been serious about someone?" I asked, knowing there was a story behind that sad look. "Ever been in love?"

"I don't know what I should call it," Nate said. "What I had, well, it wasn't exactly legal."

If only he knew how illegal mine and Colton's relationship was, he might realize he's not alone. "What do you mean not exactly legal?"

"Well, I was underage and he was older. Family friend. Yes, I was in love. It was stupid. It didn't work out because it was stupid. I don't know why I had ever thought it would."

"You said it yourself, you were in love. That's reason enough."

"It's hard to explain."

"Do you still see him?"

"I do. I told you he's a family friend so I can't exactly ignore him. But we don't fuck anymore, if that's what you're asking."

"Your family. Are you close?"

"You could say that," Nate replied. "Although it's not exactly the most functional family you've met. My father married twice. My mom was his second wife. He never stopped loving his first. His marriage with my mother lasted for barely a few months. Of course he went right back to his ex. He didn't even come to see me when I was born. But when my mom got cancer I think he felt bad for us. So, he came all the way here and gave her some money and started looking after us. He even told his wife. He has a son and two daughters from that one, so yeah, we do see each other and we're pretty friendly in general. They're nice people, even the wife, although she hates my guts."

"I'm guessing a lot of people hate your guts," I said.

He smirked. "Do you?"

"Maybe just a little."

"Well, I've never had a filter," he said, and got up and took the cup from my hand. He lifted both our empty cups and took them to the kitchen counter.

"I don't think you should change," I said. "Just to cater to someone."

"Oh believe me, I know." He walked up to me and grabbed my hand. "Get up."

So I did.

When I stood, he kissed me again. "So, what do you say we take it to the bedroom?"

"Nate, maybe we should put some brakes on this for now."

"You're having second thoughts about cheating on him."

"A little. But mainly because you're drunk."

"This is my usual state, Jason."

"I don't like fucking someone who won't even remember me the next morning."

"I thought that would be perfect for you," he said.

"Nate, we'll see each other again."

"Can I be honest?"

"Sure."

"I like you," he confessed. "I really, really like you. I mean, I've never wanted to fuck someone this much, in a very long time. I mean, I always want to fuck, but usually I don't care who's on the other end. This time, I do. I care, Jason. There's something about you. I want that, even if it's for one night."

I looked at him and smiled. "I like you too, Nate."

There was a picture of family on vacation, somewhere in Spain, on one of the side tables and it caught my eye. "Is that…"

"My family," Nate said. "Step mom and her kids. That's my older brother. And my step-sisters. They're all older than me."

"You must look up to your brother," I said. "Now that you have one."

"I guess."

Pause.

"It's complicated," he added.

"Isn't it always?"

Nate grabbed hold of a bottle of tequila from the kitchen and started pouring. He offered me a shot but I declined. I watched him, drinking alone and I wondered how often he did it. Drank alone in this huge empty house because no one was willing to give him time. Because no one had bothered to understand him. And then I reminded myself not to get so concerned with whatever his problems were. The further I stayed from all this, the better. So, I decided to leave before I changed my mind. "I'll see you around, Nate."

He said nothing.

I stopped at the door and turned to him.

"Nate. If you were my brother I'd be proud of you."

"No, you wouldn't, you'd hate my guts."

"No, Nate. I don't think anyone can truly hate you."

He scoffed. "You'd be surprised."

"Sure maybe some random people who don't get you might, but not the ones who're truly important."

There was no reply so I started to leave.

I didn't look back.

By the time I was in the street I heard the text message alert. So, I took out my phone to see who it was. It was Nate. I briefly recalled exchanging numbers during our conversation. The text said simply, "Thanks, Jason. I will never forget you. Even if we never see each other again."

I had the urge to tell him that we would see each other again, but I couldn't bring up the courage to say that. I don't know why, but I didn't even respond.

10

COLTON

Something woke me.

When I turned around I saw Jason, sitting up on his side of the bed. I could hear the faint sobbing and didn't know what to do. A part of me wanted to confront him but another part kept telling me to keep pretending to be asleep.

"Jason?"

The sobbing stopped. "Hey."

"What's wrong?"

"Nothing," he said, but I knew that was a lie. "Go back to sleep."

I turned on the bedside lamp on my side.

I saw his face.

There were tears still streaming down.

He took off his coat, tossed it aside and, still wearing the rest of the work suit, lay down next to me on the bed. "Are you okay?"

"I'm fine," I replied. "You're clearly not."

"I'm sorry, I didn't mean to unload my shit like that."

"Jason, I want you to unload your shit."

I know my brother's not exactly the most sharing person on the planet, but I can always tell when something's going on and this is one of those times. Of course the fact that he always tends to think of himself as some kind of control-freak savior, makes it impossible for him to actually let go and talk about stuff instead of keeping it all inside. I never used to get it before, but I guess now I do, a little. Sometimes I don't know how to share either, all the stuff that's been going on inside my head, I don't know how to let it out. Maybe I'm embarrassed. Maybe I'm just afraid I will let it out and he won't understand, or I'll fuck it up somehow. I realize that's not a healthy thing to do, but I figure if it doesn't come out, then there's no pressure. Not of him responding the right way and not of me having to confront things.

"Just had a strange night," Jason said.

"Strange, how?"

There was a pretty lengthy pause before he actually responded. "Just been thinking about stuff I guess."

"What kind of stuff?"

I was met with another pause, lengthier than the last. "What happened to you," he said, "was all my fault."

"Jason—"

"Let me finish, okay?" He interrupted me. "If I hadn't pissed Devyn off, if I had been careful, if I had just left with you to wherever you wanted to go, none of this would have happened and we'd still be the people we were before all this. So please, don't say it's not my fault."

I didn't know how to react, to be honest.

"And I wish I could say I'll make it up to you, I wish I could pretend everything is fine, but it's not."

"Jason, why do you sound like you're breaking up with me?"

"No," he said. "It's not that!"

"So, what then?"

"I don't think I can make it up to you," he said. "But I can do the next best thing, Colton."

"Next best thing?"

"I can't speak any more about it; the less you know the better."

"You're doing something illegal, aren't you?"

"Legality is overrated."

"No, it's not!"

He leaned over and kissed me, and I guess that lowered my defenses but I was still worried. I wished I could make him understand. That it wasn't fear for myself but fear of what might happen to him that kept me up at nights. I've seen those people, and I know what they're capable of. Not to forget that Detective Paulson sounds hell-bent to put him behind bars. Doesn't he understand that my world begins and ends with him? That if something were to happen to him I don't think I could deal with that. I'd probably go insane.

I pushed Jason onto the bed and got on top. Jason put his arms around me, and as I kissed him I felt how tense he was, and I didn't know why. "Do you want to fuck me?"

His hands were now on my face as he kissed me again. "Yes…"

I kissed him but then broke off. "How bad?"

"Bad," he said, as I unbuttoned his shirt and leaned forward to kiss his chest.

11
JASON

The bar was full of people but I spotted him rather easily.

"Hi," Nate kissed me on the cheek and smiled. Then he grabbed my crotch. "Someone's excited to see me," he grinned.

"Someone's always excited," I said, trying to make light of it but I knew that was a stupid thing to do. I was in a gay bar, not cruising, not looking for random hot guys but for one specific guy—him. It didn't get any more personal than that. I'm sure he understood it as well because he looked happy despite the fact that he wasn't drunk this time.

"I did what you asked," he spoke in my ear to cut out the noise. "Only had one martini. I've honestly never been this sober since I first started drinking in high school."

I looked around, hoping I wasn't going to see anyone I knew or anyone my brother knew. So far so good. "Can we take this someplace private?"

"What's the matter?" he said. "Afraid your husband is going to catch us?"

"Well, yeah."

"If he's here, Jason, cruising other guys, then I should be the least of your worries."

"Stop talking," I said.

He grinned, and grabbed my hand, led me towards the back by the baths. It wasn't my first time in the backrooms, but this particular bar was new to me. We finally found an empty room and got inside. There was a couch but it made me sick, thinking about all the people who must have used it prior to me. And then I wondered when I'd become that person? When had I started worrying about my surroundings when I had to fuck? Colton. That was him. Staying straight, not doing anything that you weren't supposed to do, breaking the rules only if I told him to and never of his own volition. This would creep him out. *But it never creeped you out before.*

Nate stood there, and I watched him take off his shirt and toss it on the same couch.

It was the first time I saw just how hot he was, how perfect his body looked in the dim lights. He took off his jeans and tossed them aside. Wearing only the briefs, he walked up to me. There was a strange certainty in his step, boldness, confidence, whatever you might want to call it, but it was endearing. Everything about him was, right down to his blue eyes and blonde hair. He wasn't afraid. Not about getting blown off, not about consequences. He kissed me and it was a good kiss. Promising. He even kissed in an open, self-assured way. He started unbuttoning my shirt. It was getting real. *In or out? What's it going to be, Jason?*

But there was no time to question myself when he started kissing my chest and going down towards my navel. I was still completely clueless when he opened my fly and started sucking me off, and every time he took me in, I could feel my cock in the depths of his throat. The man had zero gag reflex! My brain had officially stopped working because the blood flow was headed elsewhere. He licked my balls and my shaft, then concentrated on the tip for a long time, before putting his mouth over my cock once again and deep throating me.

He finally got off his knees and was about to kiss me when I grabbed his hair and stopped him from going through with it. He looked intently at me with those eyes. "You like it a little rough?"

"I don't think you can handle my rough," I said.

"Try me."

My hand still lodged in his hair, I gave his face a thorough glance.

I could smell his fear.

For some reason, it was exciting to me.

I let go of my grip on his hair.

"I don't want some horny slut pissing his pants," I said. "Maybe we should stick to what you're comfortable with."

He fell to his knees, folded his arms behind his back and stared up at me. "I'm a horny slut."

"We already established that."

"But I'm *your* horny slut."

My dick was throbbing.

Just thinking of the possibilities made me hard.

Without warning, I lifted my arm and slapped his beautiful face.

Hard.

My palm was still smarting from the effort so his face must have been a lot worse. The red print of my hand covered most of the left side of his face, and his eyes were all teary.

"Change your mind, whore?"

"No," his voice was hoarse.

I slowly walked up to the door and locked it, making an event out of the simple undertaking while he knelt there, not-so-patiently.

I walked back.

I grabbed his hair and pulled him up.

Pushed him towards the wall and lowered his shorts.

His ass was just as perfect as the rest of him and I could see a few crisscross marks across the cheeks, evidence that he wasn't new to playing rough.

"I'm going to give you one last chance to reconsider your decision," I said, running a hand over his exposed skin. He placed his hands on the wall and moaned when my fingers grazed over his crack.

"I'm not backing out."

I kissed the top of his shoulder.

He squirmed.

My cock was fully erect.

I put on a condom and threw some spit on one hand, ran it over my dick. I placed the tip at his hole, and rammed it in. He screamed. I'm guessing he thought I was going to let up once I was inside him, but I didn't. I kept thrusting viciously, and he kept screaming, begging me to stop. I didn't even stop when he started to cry.

It had dawned on him that this wasn't a game, and he started to get away but my hands kept him firmly in place. His frame was smaller, and he was rather fragile. Despite his need for roughness, I doubt he'd ever been in a fist fight.

Fuck, I *wanted* to keep going.

Just keep on thrusting until I came, or until he stopped breathing.

But something pulled me back.

Fuck.

Why couldn't I go through with it?

I pulled out of him and tossed the condom aside, buttoned my fly. I watched as he cried and tried to come to terms with what had just happened. "You fucking freak!" he bellowed. He was on the floor, sitting against the wall, shaking uncontrollably.

I buttoned up my shirt and tossed his clothes at him. "Put these on," I said. "Or someone might do worse than what I just did."

He stared up at me. "Just tell me why."

"What difference does it make?"

He squeezed his eyes shut and opened them again. "What did I do? Just tell me."

I went up and crouched in front of him. "That's just it, Nate. You didn't do anything."

I ceremoniously wiped the tears off his face.

"I don't understand," he said.

I reached into my pocket and handed him a folded photograph that I'd been holding on to for a long time. "Recognize the man in the picture?"

He looked at the photo. "Yes."

"Tell me who he is."

He hesitated. "That's my brother," he said. "My step brother, Devyn. But why do you have that picture?"

I took out my phone this time and showed him a picture of Colton. "You know who that is?"

He was clearly trying to remember. "He was on TV for a while," Nate said. "In a kidnapping case. Some people abducted him, tortured him."

"Raped him and beat him within an inch of his life."

"What's that got to do with me?"

I smiled. "Nothing," I said. "And everything."

I stood.

Dialed Gary's number. "Gary, I need you to come over."

I selected one of the videos, the ones those people had sent to me of Colton, and I opened it for him to see. Nate watched, in silence. Terrified. "Your brother did this," I told him, but I could tell he didn't believe me for a second.

"I don't believe you," he said, just as I'd expected. "Devyn could never…"

There was a knock on the door and I opened it.

Gary walked in.

He looked at Nate. "What do you need, Jason?"

"Take him to his brother," I said.

"No, please!" Nate's eyes begged me. "Jason, we can talk about this. If Devyn did something, I can help you. I can… we're friends!"

Gary pulled him up and forced him to put on his clothes. Then he took out his gun and placed it at Nate's ribs, the view hidden by their arms. "Come quietly,"

Gary said. "And I won't have to use this, you follow me?"

Nate didn't speak.

"Answer the fucking question, Nate!" I yelled at the top of my lungs.

He looked even more terrified now, as he complied. "I'll go quietly," he said. "Please don't hurt me." He stopped once before heading out that door. "Jason, hate isn't going to get you anywhere."

"I gave you a choice," I said. "Devyn and his friends never gave my brother even that. One minute I was in paradise and the next I was in hell, and someone had pulled the rug from under my feet."

Everything came back.

The way it had felt when I first found out Colton was missing.

The fear, the bad thoughts and the nightmares.

Between us, Colton and I had gone through enough.

It was time for someone else to feel that same pain that these bastards put us through. That was the only way my soul would find solace. The only way I could cope. We would still start that new life that we've been dreaming about, but first I want to give this to Colton.

This will be my gift to him. For surviving. For being strong enough to get through all that torture and still come out alive. For trying each day to make it work, despite the fact that it was hard for him to do so. Yes. Colton deserved this. He deserved to see his captors in worse pain than they caused him. He deserved to see them, exposed and defenseless and cowering in front of him.

    Helpless.

    As Gary took Nate out of the room, I dialed Colton's number.

    But it went straight to voicemail.

    Maybe that was a good thing.

    I'll just deliver the news in person.

    Yes.

    Justice was just around the corner.

12
COLTON

The face was familiar but it took me a while to figure out who he was.

"Detective Paulson," he said, and it certainly refreshed my memory. I tightened my hold on the shopping bags and started walking in the direction of the café, hoping the detective would leave me alone.

"Are you stalking me?"

"Can we go sit somewhere and talk?" he asked, walking right next to me. "It's important."

I was glad he couldn't see my eyes through the sunglasses or he would have seen the anger. I wasn't just annoyed, I burned with rage. It was an invasion of privacy. But it wasn't worth angering him so I played along. "Sure."

We sat in the café and I looked around. The place was bursting with people who didn't care who we were. "Well, what did you want to talk to me about?"

"You have any idea what your brother's up to?"

"Jason?"

"Any other brothers I don't know of?"

I bit my tongue. "Jason hasn't been up to anything. Except taking care of me."

"Let's cut to the chase," Paulson said. "I know your parents died. I know your brother has been taking care of you since then, you feel like you need to be loyal to him, family and all that. I get it."

"Do you?" I shot back. "Because it seems to me like you're constantly pressing me for things I have no clue about."

"Listen to me, Colton. Jason saved you, rescued you from that place. I know that. And I know you'll keep denying it but it doesn't matter. I'm glad you're back. But that's not why I'm here, son."

"Why are you here?"

"I'm here because what your brother is doing now, you're the only one who can save him."

For some reason when the Detective said that I believed him. Not the part that I was the only one who could save him but the part where he told me Jason was up to something. Because even I knew that was true. What the hell had Jason gotten himself into now?

"What do you think he's up to?"

"Son. He's holding Devyn and his friends captive. Two days ago, Devyn's half-brother went missing, and I have a pretty good idea your brother had something to do with it."

It surprised me but only because I felt betrayed.

Jason had been lying to me, obviously.

I couldn't understand why he was doing this to me. After everything we've been through, how could he let me go through this?

"I don't know what you're talking about, Detective."

"Come on, son. Don't be that way."

"Excuse me?"

"These people are human beings with family! Kids, wives, brothers, sisters… that Nate kid? He's about as old as you, Colton."

"I honestly don't know what you're talking about."

"I believe you, son. I do. But maybe you can help me find out more?"

"Why would I do that, Detective?" I retorted. "Because you sat with me in some café and called me *son* a few times? That ploy's a little obvious, don't you think? Not to forget really old."

"Look, we don't have a lot of time. I can't spend my time convincing you about the truth. But sooner or later, this is going to blow up. Jason is all alone in this. He might fight one or two factions, but he can't fight everyone. A person with no friends? Is that really who he wants to be? There are people gunning for him as we speak, Colton. Dangerous people. If you don't help him, then he will end up like your parents. Dead. Is that what you want?"

I couldn't stop thinking about the Detective's words but I tried to stay calm. "I'm curious," I said. "What exactly do you expect me to do here?"

"Talk some sense into your brother," Paulson replied. "Tell him that I'm not the enemy. We can cut a deal with him, he will get a shortened sentence. In a few years he'll be out and you'll be with him again. Don't you think that's better than him dying stupidly by some enemy bullet?"

I had to take time to think.

The Detective's spiel could have been a ploy, but I knew he wasn't going to leave me alone unless I agreed to do something. Maybe I could pretend to help him. Just to get him off my back and buy some time, so I could talk to Jason about the whole thing. Maybe convince him to step off the fucking ledge. "What do you want me to do?"

Paulson reached inside his jacket and took out his business card. "I know you probably lost the one I gave you before," he said.

I took it from him and placed it inside my jeans pocket.

"Secure line."

"Okay."

"Colton, you need to confront him."

"I don't even know if you're telling the truth or making this up just to get me to go along with some scheme of yours to get us both in trouble."

"I know where he's hiding the captives," Paulson said.

"You know?" I said. "Then why haven't you arrested him?"

"Because search warrants are hard to come by for someone as clean slate and connected as your brother,"

Paulson said. "Colton, listen to me. I don't care about arresting your brother, believe it or not, that's not what I'm interested in."

"So what are you interested in?"

"If he returns those people, if he lets them go unscathed," Paulson said, "I'm willing to look the other way."

"And will your other cop friends look the other way too?"

"This place is a joke. This whole town, it thrives on corruption. I've never been part of that cycle. And I thought that was a good thing, but a decade in this same job, I know things now that I never knew before. I know this place isn't about to change any time soon. I know these criminals will always have the upper hand because this system is corrupted. But I'm done being watchdog. For once, I want to use the system. Even if it's to get those people to their families."

"So you're doing this from the goodness of your heart, is that it?"

"I'm doing this as a *fuck you* to everyone in the system."

"I don't believe you."

"I'm not asking for your belief," Paulson said. "I'm asking you to go to your brother and talk to him. That's it. No catch."

"What's the address?"

"How will you get there?"

"What do you care?"

"I care because if you're going to take one of your brother's lackeys with you, that's not going to be fruitful. Jason might get spooked then, and we would be left with nothing. He must have a Plan B. We don't want that. What if he tries to kill someone?"

"Fine. I'll be careful."

After some initial hesitation, Paulson handed me the address.

13

JASON

The old cottage was in the middle of nowhere.

As kids Colton and I had come here once, on what I now know to be a ruse. Father brought us here because he was under attack by a bunch of gang people, and he always treated this place like a safe-house. It wasn't our usual vacation but that summer we had a lot of fun. My uncle and his family were also vacationing with us, and I remember we never wanted to go home. I must have been about six.

Turning father's safe-house into a hideout wasn't my initial plan but because the place where I had been keeping the captives had been burned down, it was the only option.

One by one, I had brought them all here.

Today, it was time for a new addition.

Nate Taylor.

The guy who made the mistake of trusting me and was now in deep shit.

It was the first time after a long time that I felt in control again.

It was strange but sometimes control is the one thing you can hang onto that feels like power. It feels like something that will last forever. Ever since Dad died, I had made sure I always had control. Once you know what people are truly capable of, it's not that hard to understand the appeal of total dominance. One tiny little problem and your brother might have to pay for it for the rest of his life. In a way I was paying for it too. No one understood that but it's true. Maybe someday I will be able to make Colton understand, but for now I was alone. I never involved my brother in all of this because I don't know how he'll react. I know I have to face him, sooner or later, but for now, I'm fine with delaying the end. I know it's merely postponing the inevitable and kind of useless, but life isn't perfect and neither are plans.

Gary closed the door and it clicked shut.

He pushed Nate toward his brother, Devyn, who was tied to a chair.

His face was messed up, thanks to the many beatings he had taken at my hands and at my men's hands, and I knew he barely had the strength in him to stand. We never gave these bastards much food, just enough to keep them alive. The beatings meant they had broken bones and their bodies were fucked up.

Devyn saw Nate and the look of fear on his face was priceless.

Gary was still handling Nate, roughly.

"Jason," Devyn stared at me. There were a million questions in his eyes but he never asked them.

"I know," I said, grinning. "Think of this as the worst family reunion."

Devyn still looked like he was in shock.

"Did you really think you could hide him from me?"

"Jason, he's done nothing…"

"Not yet," I said. "But he will."

"I don't… understand."

Without giving Devyn a response I went up to Nate. I pressed my gun to his head. "You know why they took my brother?"

Nate shook his head 'no.'

"They knew about me and him," I said. "That Colton and I…" it was the first time I was saying this in front of Gary but I knew I couldn't act like I gave a shit. *Control.* "Were together."

As I expected, Gary didn't react.

Maybe he already knew.

Or if he didn't know for sure, he might have suspected it.

The guy knew us since we were little, there wasn't much we could hide from someone like that. I tried not to think about it and instead focused on what was going on. More importantly, what I knew was about to happen. It was strange, wasn't it? That I was the only one who knew what was going to happen? The only one who had control over how this ends?

Unsurprisingly, Nate didn't look appalled.

"What's the matter, Nate?" I asked. "You seem astoundingly okay with all this information?"

"I just don't think it's my business what two consenting adults decide to do."

"Maybe you're more open minded than your brother, Nate. Or maybe, you have a secret too."

"There's no secret."

"Of course there is," I taunted. "The secret is hidden away in the flash drive that stays underneath your pillow."

I brought out the blue stick and showed it to the room. "Do we have a laptop, Gary?"

"Of course, sir. I'll go bring it now."

"Thank you."

"No!" Nate protested. The bastard was actually worried about his brother finding out. I realized I didn't even have to play the stuff on that drive to get what I needed.

I turned to Nate. "If you want me to spare your brother the sight of you jerking off to his videos, then tell him exactly what you did."

Nate had tears in his eyes.

He looked like he wanted to die of shame.

He wasn't making eye contact with Devyn.

"Nate, what's he talking about?" Devyn inquired.

"Yeah Nate," I said. "Tell him."

Nate barely managed to get the words out. "A couple of years ago, I set up a surveillance camera in your place," he said. "In a couple of locations."

"Why would you do that?" Devyn seemed pissed.

There was a pause before Nate finally came out with the truth. "Devyn, I wanted to see you," he said. "I was always attracted to you. I know it's crazy, sleazy even. You hate that stuff but I can't help it, Dev!"

"You fucking piece of shit," Devyn said, and it was obvious he was having trouble keeping his anger in check. "I loved you like a brother and you did this! You violated me! You and your trash mother, you're both nothing but trouble. Mom always told me that but I kept thinking she was just being biased. Thought maybe if I loved you, then you wouldn't turn out to be a whore like her!"

Instead of defending his mother, Nate was quiet and weeping.

"Dev, I'm sorry!" he said.

It made me realize he actually loved that stupid fucked up brother of his, and he must have truly cared about him. "Maybe you find your little brother attractive too, Devyn? He's hot, don't you think? Would it be so bad to just accept it?"

"Fuck you," Devyn cursed. "Incest makes me sick! And incestuous bastards make me sicker!"

"Methinks thou dost protest too much."

"Fuck you, Jason!"

I had to laugh.

But when I was done, I grabbed Nate and started hitting him.

I gave him a few blows in the ribs, then switched to his face until it was cut and bleeding. He was screaming and in pain, but that wasn't the best part.

The best part was watching Devyn cringe.

The last blow to Nate's face, made his nose bleed and the blood sprayed all over Devyn.

"Stop!" Devyn said.

My work here is done, folks.

"What's the matter?" I said. "You said you hated incestuous people, but what's this now? Are you asking me to spare this little incestuous shit?"

"Just let him go, he hasn't done anything!"

"I will," I said. "But first you have to admit you love him."

"He's my brother, of course I love him!"

"He's your half-brother," I reminded him. "Born from a woman who ruined your parents' marriage."

"None of that is his fault."

"Maybe not. But I've yet to see two half-brothers being so in love."

"Will it make you happy?" Devyn asked. "If I said I loved him? Will you let us go?"

"Of course not," I replied. "But I will consider letting *him* go."

Devyn closed his eyes, teared up, opened them again.

He looked at Nate but there was no eye contact. "I love you, Nate."

Nate was crying now, more than before. "I'm sorry," he whined.

"It's okay," Devyn said. "You'll get out of here, okay? I'll make sure of it. Nothing's going to happen to you."

"Isn't that sweet!" I mocked. "But you can't promise baby bro anything like that unless you do what I say."

"What's it you want?"

My gun still pointed at him, I grabbed Nate by the shoulder and pushed him to his knees. He was on the floor, poised in front of Devyn. "Give big brother a blowjob, Nate. And not the kind that you give to someone to get it over with. The kind you gave me the other night."

Devyn looked like someone had just snatched the world from under him. "You bastard."

I grinned. "Fucking is a mutual act," I said. "It's not like I raped your brother!" I paused. "At least not at first!"

There was a lot that Devyn must have wanted to say then, but he didn't.

"Come on, Devyn. Convince your brother," I said.

Devyn looked at me with pleading eyes. "Please, Jason, you made your point. You have us, you took your revenge! Please let us go. Don't do this."

I slowly walked up to Devyn. "You know how many times my brother pleaded in front of you all?" I said. "Begged? You beat him to death, it took me months Devyn, *months* to get him to walk on his own two feet! This from a guy who used to fight with me all the time over you! Asking me why I wouldn't trust you. Telling me you were a good person, even when I knew that was a lie. Because that's who he was! He wanted to believe in good. In humanity. He didn't deserve the cruelty you put him through." I waited for a reply but there was nothing. Devyn looked defeated. That was what I had wanted all along but I wasn't satisfied. Not by far. I guess my appetite for revenge was starting to surprise even me.

"Jason—"

"Do it," I said. "Do it, or what you did to Colton will seem like mercy when I'm done with Nate."

Devyn finally made eye contact. He looked right into Nate's eyes. "It's okay, Nate. Just do what he says, okay? Sooner you do it, the sooner you can get out of this."

"I can't..." Nate cried.

Nate might have been jacking off to Devyn in fantasy, but in reality he was scared. I saw it in his eyes. It was the same fear I had seen in Colton's eyes once. I knew what it was. Making fantasies come true isn't always as simple as it sounds. Reality can be hard. It helped that Colton and I were so synchronized. It also helped that Colton always took my lead. Fuck, I loved that stupid little shit more than I loved my parents. It wasn't something disgusting. It was pure and beautiful. But people like Devyn made it ugly. With their own ridiculous hang-ups and their hate. Well, I couldn't change the world, but I could change a few of them.

The door opened and two of the security men walked in, dragging someone with them. "Sir, we found him in the surveillance room."

"Colton," I was surprised to see him. "What're you doing here?"

"Jason, I came to help you. Tell you that your so-called secret location isn't secret anymore. But you… Fuck, Jason I don't even know who you are."

I gestured to the men to leave.

Then I turned to my brother. "How long have you been watching me?"

"Long enough to know that you're no different than them!"

"Colton, you can't be a lamb and fight wild animals!"

"So, become a monster to hurt the monster? That's your solution?"

"You say that like it's a bad thing," I said, a bit annoyed that I was having to fight my brother too. This should have been easy, I was doing this for him, but nothing with Colton was ever easy. I walked up to him and touched his face. "Come with me," I said. "Let's talk."

I told Gary to keep an eye on those two and came outside the cottage to talk to Colton. The minute we were outside he started fuming. "Did you know the cops know about this place?"

"So we'll switch."

"Fuck, don't you get it?" he yelled. "This isn't a joke."

I went up to him and kissed him. "Baby, I know you're worried. But there's nothing to worry about. I have everything under control."

He looked up at me. "You love me, don't you?"

"Yes."

"More than anything?"

"Of course!"

"Then do what I'm asking you to do. Please. Just leave all this behind. Come with me. We'll go, leave the country, change our names, get new identities…"

"We will. We'll do all that, Colton. Just as soon as I'm done with those bastards."

He shoved me. "Why can't you just let it go?"

"How can I let it go?" I said. "I'll never forget it. What they did to my brother…"

"I'm standing right here, Jason, quit talking about me in the past tense!"

There was the sound of gunshots and then a blast. Followed by screams.

Colton looked rattled. "What was that?"

"I don't know," I said, taking out my gun from the holster and making sure it was loaded. "But it looks like we might be under attack."

"Under attack?"

"Did you bring your gun?"

"No! Why the hell would I bring it?"

"Colton, I gave you that thing for a reason! I told you to keep it on you at all times!"

"I forgot, okay?"

"Just… stay behind me, okay?" I said and led our way through the forest. There were more gunshots, more screaming, and I quickened our pace. We ran into someone. "Andy?" he was one of my men. Andy opened his mouth to speak but a bullet tore through him and I saw him falling face-first into the ground. Before we could run, a man came out from behind the tree., carrying a rifle. I would have taken a shot at him but someone yelled, "Drop your weapon, Hamilton! And we won't hurt your brother."

I turned to find a bunch of strange men surrounding us and one of them had his weapon pointed at Colton. The math was simple. There were just too many of them. I lowered my gun to the ground and dropped it. The men dragged us both to a clearing…

14

COLTON

I was on the ground.

Blood streaming into my eyes.

There was the smell of cold, damp earth, and I saw them, grabbing Jason... and then there was a gunshot. I forced my eyes open. Jason, was on the ground, and Grey's gun was still pointed at him.

"No..." I cried.

But I couldn't move.

I watched them, kicking Jason into a six-foot ditch and then the men started scooping dirt from a mound next to the ditch, and they started filling the ditch with the same dirt...

"Noooooo!" I screamed.

My heart was in a million little pieces, and something was stomping on it.

I was paralyzed but someone grabbed me and dragged me away...

15
COLTON

Maybe it was a sign of my growing insanity. What else could this overwhelming urge to laugh in the dark be? I've been despondent, I've been rebellious, and then I came to accept my fate. Now that Jason was no longer around, I had no reason to hold on to this pointless existence anyway. Even if Devyn did give me my freedom—I mean, I'm guessing Devyn is behind all this—I'd give it right back to him and beg him to just kill me instead. What was the point of living without Jason?

Another cough starting deep inside my chest, wracked its way up my throat and rattled my shivering body. Or maybe I wasn't shivering, and maybe it wasn't a cough. Maybe it was the laughter I kept hearing, my laughter. Laughter at the cosmic joke that was on me, a joke I couldn't escape.

There was a time when everything was perfect. It had been a short time, but I had held perfection in my hands. That was more than many people had in their lifetimes, so I could hold on to that. Hopefully, wherever I'm headed, I'd get to see Jason again. He's waiting for me there, I know he is, and he's getting things ready for me. Mustard hotdogs and endless summer days, just him and me and no one else.

That sounded like heaven to me, which is why I'm sure that couldn't exist in this life. I wished for the millionth time that Devyn would just kill me already. Or if he didn't have the fucking guts to do it, give me something to do it for him. For both of us. It would be the ultimate mercy he could give me. Which is why he was holding death just outside my grasp. When I die, his hold over me dies with me. We both knew that.

So he kept delaying the inevitability of my sweet release. If I could just hold out, get myself through these last few hours, hopefully death would fold me in its arms and deliver me to Jason, where we would only know peace.

Death was there with me, he hovered just out of reach, his presence a promise of the relief he brought. I just had to hold on a little while longer and he would take me home.

Hold on, I told myself as the door's latch clanged and the hinges creaked open.

What did Devyn have in store for me now? Waterboarding? No, that's not creative enough. "Amputation?" I asked the shadow standing in the light. "Want to tear me limb from limb?" My throat scratched from dryness, and I should've kept quiet. But I was done pleading, I was done hoping. I was the most dangerous person on earth—someone who was ready to die.

My eyes adjusted to the light shining into the room enough to make out the silhouette framed in the door wasn't Devyn's skinny frame. I couldn't be bothered to figure out who it was either. Hopefully the Grim Reaper, but I didn't hold out much hope. The person didn't answer me, just stood there with a distinct bend to his hip and hand on his side…

I resisted the surge of hope that threatened to descend over me and pulled the cloak of despair tighter, not allowing my hopes to soar. But when the person spoke, I couldn't help but accept the tiniest bit of relief as his voice washed over me.

"Seems like I was right all along."

"Uncle Dave?" My voice rasped in the quiet of the damp room.

"Was I right, Colton?"

"Please help me."

My uncle didn't move toward me. "I was right."

"About what?" I finally asked when he still didn't move.

"You fucked everything up."

"No, I didn't," I said, as things fell into place. "You did," I yelled with strength I wasn't sure was coming from. "You're with Devyn, aren't you? How else could he come up with this and bankroll it all?"

Dave stepped out of the door and walked into the room. He wore dress pants and a button-down shirt. He fiddled with the cuffs of the shirt. "Well, fuck me, congratulations." Dave started unbuttoning the shirt and kicked off his shoes. "It took you long enough."

"You had Jason killed too, didn't you? Why?" I kicked at him, he was that close to me. But I could hardly get my frigid knee off the ground. "He was your favorite!"

"That is another thing you can lay at your door," Dave said and pulled his shirt out of his pants. Why was he undressing in this cold room of hell? "It's part of what you fucked up. So you can lay that blame square on your pathetic little shoulders."

"Fuck you," I said, refusing to believe him.

"You killed Jason. If you weren't such a pervert, fucking your brother every chance you got. He could've led a normal life. Carried on the legacy. Made us all proud. How the fuck do you think I could introduce the two of you to people? To presidents, to world leaders?"

"Jason didn't care about that."

"You're right," Dave said and kicked his shoes off. "He didn't, you made sure of that. All he had in his mind was fucking your ass. That right there was all he cared about."

"So you killed him?" I screamed the words with what little strength I had left. Dave unbuckled his pants and slid them to the floor.

"No, bitch. You did. You killed him the day you didn't fucking get the message to fuck off out of his life. This is all on you," he yelled and stepped out of his pants. Standing before me in his briefs and knee-high socks with his beer belly and skinny thighs made me want to start laughing all over again.

"What? Not what you're used to? You used to getting finer dick than this?" Dave grabbed his crotch and pulled it toward me. "I bet you are. Filthy slut. I've seen the videos. You're a fucking natural by now. So I told Devyn, no use in letting the bitch die before I get to taste what my investment created. I paid to have you turned into this, I might as well get some reward for it."

"You're a fucking pig. I always knew that, but there was a time Jason believed in you. You betrayed him," I said, trying to get our uncle to see the level of his betrayal. "But you never cared about Jason either. He was just a means to an end to you."

Dave walked to me slowly. "You know…" He kept staring at me without blinking, drinking in my helplessness, my fear. "I always carried a torch for your mother. Fuck, I wanted to shove her across the table every time I saw her and give it to her like I knew my brother never would. She deserved to get fucked properly in her life at least once. It's one of my biggest regrets, you know." He kept staring at me and I pushed myself deeper into the cold, wet corner of the smelly room.

"If I had been the man I am today, you can bet these last thirty minutes in life that I would've showed her what a true man is."

Dave was so close to me now that I saw his lips purse together as he sneered at me. "But I guess you will have to do. If I close my eyes, I might be able to imagine that is your mom's pussy I'm pounding into when I show *you* what a real man is."

"Fuck off!"

Dave grabbed my hair and pulled me to my knees. My fists hitting into his sides were ineffectual, even though I put what little strength I had behind it.

"I'm going to fuck you so hard you're going to wish for Gray and Logan's dick when I'm done with you." Dave pulled back his arm and sank it into my abdomen, winding me and letting me drop to the ground as I coughed my lungs out through my throat. "You ruined everything, fucker. Now I'll return the favor."

He bent down next to me and pulled my wrists forward. I didn't even struggle, didn't have it in me anymore. Dave dragged me to the door and let me sink in a puddle of exhaustion. He hooked a pair of handcuffs through an exposed utility pipe near the wall and placed it tightly over my wrists, locking me in place.

"This is the closest I'll ever get to fucking your mother, and you can be damn sure I'm going to make it count. Pissing me off even more won't do you any favors."

"If you think I care, then you're more deluded than I thought. I'm dead. Do your worst, pig."

Dave hit me in the gut, breaking the numb coldness that had set in. The sting stayed with me as he lifted me up on my knees and positioned his dick at my ass. I closed my eyes and gritted my teeth at the anticipated invasion. There was a time when I opened my ass up slowly to accept Jason in there. He'd sink into me, and the moment I pulled him deeper he'd close his eyes and arch his neck, swallowing slowly as pleasure washed over him. His Adam's apple would bob as the dry swallow clicked his throat and I had to pull deep inside of me to not reach up and fucking suck on his neck.

Dave sunk into me.

Every time when Jason fucked me, I kept my cool and resisted the urge to lift my head and kiss his neck. I wish now I had kissed that Adam's apple. Felt the vibrations of pleasure that ran through it as Jason hovered over me, filling me with his swollen dick. Why hadn't I?

Dave shoved in deep, pushing me forward and bumping my head against the wall while building up a rhythm. Maybe my concussion would kill me, I might pass out first and then just disappear into eternity.

When Jason would open his eyes after the initial rush of pleasure washed over him, he'd stare at me with eyes drowning in lust. That was the moment I was sure that no one else had ever pulled that reaction out of him. Not any silly girl with dreams of landing a rich, eligible bachelor to marry her and give her a fantasy life, and not some slutty guy desperate for the attention of a born dominator.

Dave wrapped his hand in my matted hair and pulled my head back as he shoved deeper into me. I was trying very hard to not be in the moment, but Dave was managing to pull me out of my memory of Jason. I didn't want to let him succeed, but my non-reaction to his rape was pissing him off and driving him to get more vicious.

"Bitch," Dave said through thrusts. "Fucking bitch. You're a dog, aren't you? No, you're not. You're a horse. That's right. You were born to be ridden. Weren't you?"

I said nothing, allowing my body to take the bruising rhythm of Dave's fucking. My soft cries encouraged Dave as he shoved into me harder.

"Fuck, no wonder he was addicted to you."

I closed my eyes again, imagining Jason in his black underwear, lying next to me and thinking of ways to get me to smile. I'd been so over life then. Even though it was a shitty time, it was actually one of the best moments in my life and I'd give anything to relive that. To be that clean, that safe with the only person who I ever really loved.

"Pig," Dave grunted.

His dick was swelling between my thighs and I hoped it would all soon be over.

"I should've fucked your mother every day of her life. I'd have given her a pair of real men for sons. My sons would have been ten times the men you and Jason were. Fuck, I should've just fucked her when I had the chance. At least I'm fucking her over now, and my useless brother, too."

"Fuck you," I said softly, barely above a whisper.

Dave leaned forward, without breaking his rhythm. "My only regret is getting to your ass this late. It's loose now, fucked beyond its years. I should've gotten to you when you were still tight." He grunted in my ear, disgusting me with his foul breath. "But you weren't tight from the day you turned thirteen, were you slut? No, Jason made sure of that."

"Fuck you," I said again, having nothing else left in me.

"I think you've got it wrong, it's you being fucked here." Dave laughed at his wit, and if I cared enough I'd have rolled my eyes.

He wiggled his hips obnoxiously, poking his dick at different angles inside of me. This led him to wrapping a sweaty hand over my bruised dick and squeezing tight. He pulled downward, and my ass locked around his dick. I hated responding like that, but I wasn't in control of my body anymore. Had I ever been?

The pain pulled me out of my reverie and pushed me into the moment I didn't want to be in.

"That's better," he wheezed. "Jason begged for his life, you know." Dave let go of my hair. He kept on tugging on my dick and balls heavy-handedly, making my ass crown around his dick. "He begged me to let him live. Not for him, I think. No, he wanted to be around to try and save you, take care of you. Know what I told him before I fed him his own dick?"

I hung my head, wishing I could put my fingers in my ear and lock this bastard's voice out of my head.

"I told him I was going to enjoy this, right here. I told him I'd make it slow for you as I fed you my dick, choked you on my dick. And I promised him that I would make this the worst day of your life, which by the sounds of it is quite a tall order. He was crying by the time I fucking ended it for him. Actually crying, can you believe that?"

I couldn't take anymore. I was just ready to join him in whatever hell he was waiting for me. I collapsed forward, crushing Dave's hand under me and feeling his dick pull out all the way.

"Hell, no," he said. "You don't get to check out on me. Not till I'm done with you."

Dave leaned over me and undid the cuffs, freeing my arms from the pipes. He was just as confident as I was that I wouldn't try anything, and I proved us both right by sagging down into a pile of bones.

He turned me over and slapped my face, pulling me back into the room with him. He wore the smug smile I'd seen him carry around when he concluded a business deal with Jason, the type of smile where he felt he had done one over on someone. He was fucking his brother's son to death, and he felt like he got one over on him. On

Jason. On my mom. On me. And he did. He got one over on all of us.

He slapped me again, and again, and again, but I didn't do anything to shuck off the beating. So he pulled on my ruined nipples, which made me wince but nothing more.

Dave didn't get it. The worst thing he could do to me was to leave me alone in that dingy room. The darkness, the aloneness and emptiness of the room was the worst type of torture I could be subjected to, and that I had been subjected to. Having him here, even spearing me with his dick like he was at that moment, was more of a comfort to me than being left alone with my terrifying thoughts.

"I promised Jason I would make you cry," Dave said, pushing into me harder. "That's just what I intend to do."

He slammed into me so hard that I felt winded. My back was scraped raw from meshing with the dirt on the floor. I couldn't breathe, and I wanted it all to just be over.

Dave wrapped his hand around my dick and balls again and pulled for all his might. Did he want to castrate me with the force of his hand alone? I moved my head, trying to get away from the dripping water falling on my cheeks. Only it wasn't water, it was my tears, tears I didn't even know I had physically left in me. Surely my body had to be dehydrated beyond measure by now.

Dave leaned into me and slammed two, three more times, then crushed my dick in his hand as his own dick swelled between my thighs. Spurt after spurt of semen hit the walls of my ass, a sensation I had become all too familiar with in recent times, and I prayed for it to be finally over now.

He let go and sank down on top of me, crushing me under his weight. Catching his breath, he pushed off me and looked me up and down. "I so want to kill you right now," he said slowly. "But I think you have another session left in you, don't you? I'll just leave you here alone in this room that is fitting to someone of your stature, and maybe I'll be back. Or I'll just leave you to wither away slowly. Guess you'll have to find out."

With that he got up and left me in a pile of brokenness. Dave gathered his clothes and walked to the door.

"I wish you could've seen Jason beg the only time in his life."

I think I had died and this was hell.

16
COLTON

The haze finally lifted.

But of course that wasn't a good thing.

I wanted to just lie there and wait for my death, but I knew sometimes death was a relief that you could never find. These bastards might have plans of keeping me here longer. Even if they did decide to kill me it wouldn't be on my terms. It would be something out of a horror movie, I was certain of that.

But the worst fear was of having to see Dave again.

Having to face that was awful.

It's not as though he and I had ever been close, but he had been my *uncle*. The man who was supposed to protect us and take care of us after our father's death.

Instead, he had betrayed us in a way that most strangers, hell, even most enemies wouldn't.

My hand hurt.

A lot of things hurt, so it was hard to pinpoint that particular ache, but I noticed there was a nail sticking out of it. I had to pry the nail out with my teeth. It must have been lying around the room somewhere, on the floor. I heard the sound of approaching footsteps and sat upright to one side of the room. I held the nail in one hand, the sharp end sticking out. It wasn't much, but I was sure repeated stabbing would make even a nail a rather dangerous weapon. If the person was close enough to me I could do it.

Dave walked in.

I saw him locking the door using a key that he dropped back into his pocket.

"How're you doing, pig?"

I almost lunged for him, but didn't.

Instead I looked up at him and murmured some random words.

"What?" Dave tried to figure out what I was trying to say.

Of course there was nothing to figure out, I was merely repeating words that didn't make any sense. But

Dave didn't know that. He came closer, leaned forward so he could hear better, and that was my chance. I drove the nail in his face. Before he knew what was happening I had successfully rattled him. I kept stabbing him until he started to scream and tried to get away from me. I managed to grab hold of his gun and I pointed it at him.

I wanted to shoot.

I should have.

Instead I found his keys and forced him to sit on the floor. Then I broke out of that room and locked him in. Outside, it was chaos.

There was an exit right outside that room where I could see people struggling, firing shots, trying to keep Jason's men in line.

I ran.

I went as far as a clearing in the forest and that's when I had to stop.

One of the enemy men was holding a weapon at me. "Go back, Hamilton."

I had no idea who he was but apparently he knew me. I held up my gun at him in response. "Let me go," I said. "Or I'll blow up your fucking face."

The bushes moved, and about four more men came out, all carrying weapons, assault rifles mostly but one or two handguns.

"Give up, Hamilton."

I didn't.

Couldn't.

"We have orders to kill you on sight, kid," the man said. "I'm being generous. Drop the weapon, and give up. It's what your brother did."

And all of them, every single one, laughed.

"My brother didn't give up!" I yelled. "He was stabbed in the back! It's the only way you could get to him!"

"Right," he said. "As if we didn't all see him begging for his life!"

Rage burned inside me.

My body was shaking.

Jason.

Jason was dead.

And these men were responsible.

I cocked my handgun, and pressed the trigger.

There was the sound of someone screaming their lungs out and I realized that was me. I drowned those bastards in a spray of bullets until there was nothing but silence.

The tears wouldn't stop.

I looked around at the death and devastation around me and I knew that I was part of it. I had half a mind to put the same gun to my head and pull that trigger once more, but I didn't do it. Instead, I went over to their dead leader and poked him with one foot to make sure he was really dead. He was. So were the others. I threw down Dave's gun and picked up the rifle that man was carrying. Armed with the weapon, I started walking back to the cottage.

17

COLTON

It's strange, but once you kill someone, once you reach that level of violence, everything changes.

Nothing is the same. I felt as though there was a strong liquid coursing through my veins, like a drug, firing me up. It wasn't just excitement, no it was more than that—it was strength—like the final adrenaline rush in a fight with a difficult opponent.

I decided to use that rush in my favor.

The first thing I did was to get to one of the other locked rooms, where they were keeping the captives. There was an entire wing dedicated to it. The same place where Devyn had been held, where Jason must have kept Logan, Grey and Ash...

I shot the two guards guarding a room and went inside. "Gary?"

He looked up, his face was cut and swollen in places, but he seemed fine otherwise. He seemed surprised to see me. I cut off his ties and freed him. When we came out of the room, he picked up the rifles the guards were carrying and loaded them.

"Gary, you're free," I said. "You can just go. You don't have to do this."

"That's nice of you, sir. But I made some promises to your father that I intend to keep."

I couldn't believe my luck.

Someone was actually willing to help.

"Thank you."

Room after room, we found more people, willing to join us and I didn't know if it was because of Gary or my brother, or my father's legacy, but they were all willing to help. "That's the last room," Gary reminded me. "Be careful. It could be a trap."

I took a deep breath and opened the lock.

"Here goes nothing," I said and stepped in.

Unlike the other rooms which all had some kind of light source, however small, this room was dark. I couldn't see a thing. Thankfully, one of the men had salvaged a flashlight from one of the dead guards. When I shined the light on the face of the captive, I had trouble making sense of what I was seeing.

"Colton, is that you?" the captive tried to keep his eyes open despite the flashlight but he was having trouble doing it.

"Jason?" I couldn't believe my eyes. Or my ears. But that was Jason's face and that was definitely his voice. "They told me you were dead!"

"They told me *you* were dead!"

"Sir," Gary stepped in. "I hate to be the bearer of bad news, but we don't have much time. The sooner we get out of here the better."

"Gary?" Jason said. "Is that you?"

"Yes sir. Mr. Hamilton rescued me. He rescued all of us."

Jason stared at me. "You did?"

I used the knife I had confiscated earlier to cut through Jason's ties. "Shut up."

The minute Jason was free from the ties, he hugged me.

He kept kissing me repeatedly. "I thought you were dead, Colton! *Fuck!*"

Then he looked at Gary and hugged him too. "So good to see you, Gary!"

We walked out of the room and Jason saw the dozen men waiting outside, their weapons ready to shoot anyone who walked by. He thwacked my back, annoyingly hard. "You rescued all these people," he said. "And you just led an army of men to save me. Looks like you're not that much different from me after all."

I wish he hadn't said that.

He didn't even know how right he was about me.

About us.

It was almost like there was some latent creature always sitting inside me that had just been woken. It seemed like that creature was the one in control, and I was merely going through the motions. How could that be a good thing? But my brother clearly thought that it was.

"Hello Jason," I heard a familiar voice.

18
COLTON

"Nice seeing you again, Devyn."

My brother's words were thick with sarcasm.

But it was useless because Devyn's men were surrounding us. "If you go quietly, I promise not to break any bones," Devyn said. "Well, not yet anyway."

"Did anyone tell you your sense of humor sucks balls?"

"Keep talking and I won't leave you with a mouth to talk with," Devyn warned and I hoped Jason would heed it for once. They led us to a massive room, tied me, Jason and Gary to chairs and took the others away.

"Here's the thing," Jason said. "You let us go and I will tell you how you can save your ass and get out of here."

"Why would I want to do that?" Devyn asked.

"Because this place is about to blow up," Jason said.

He was bluffing. Right?

He had to be.

I'm sure he was saying this to play with Devyn's head. "There's a minefield of C4 under the four main wings," Jason said. "I know how to disarm it. Even Gary doesn't know anything about that."

"You're lying," Devyn said, but I knew he was faking the calm.

"Want to see for yourself?" Jason said. "All you have to do is wait for..." he checked his watch dramatically. "Fifteen minutes and twenty-two seconds."

Devyn angrily pressed the gun to Jason's head. "I'm going to blow your head off long before I get blown up."

"Look at that folks," Jason said. "Devyn Taylor being a fucking martyr!" He turned to Devyn. "You can be a martyr all you want. But your brother is in the same building. And I really doubt that he wants to die anytime soon."

"Yeah?" Devyn said. "What about your brother? Are you really okay with him dying?"

Jason looked at me. "You already killed us once," he said. "You can do it again."

I kept my mouth shut. I knew there was a point to everything Jason was saying. I was going to just wait and see what it was.

It was clear Jason had convinced Devyn. "Tell me where the charges are hidden."

"I can show you," Jason replied.

Devyn laughed. "Do you think I'm that dumb?"

"Clearly you are," Jason said. "Those charges need to be disarmed and I'm the only one who can do it, I just told you that."

The door opened and one of the guards stepped in. "They found C4," he said to Devyn. "But it's complicated. None of the men are capable of disarming it."

Jason stared at Devyn. "Told you I wasn't lying."

"Shut up and let me think!" Devyn said angrily.

"There's no time," Jason said. "This place is rigged with C4 that's about to kill us all."

"So you do care about your own life."

"Fine. I care! Okay? I fucking care, now please take me to the charges."

Devyn turned to the men. "Take him," he pointed to Jason. Jason winked at me. I hoped that was a good sign.

When they left, Gary whispered to me, "This place is rigged but it's not going off in fifteen minutes."

Well, I suppose that was a relief.

"It's going off in one hour."

"Eh, peace of mind is overrated anyway," I said.

But Gary wasn't done. "You don't understand," he said. "Jason doesn't know how to disarm that thing. The man who did for us, Fenton, he's the explosives expert and he was one of the first to die."

"So, Jason's making this up? Why?"

"Beats me."

And then it hit me. "Wait. Jason wanted them out of the room. He knew we'd discuss this, that I would find out. This room, Gary, is it possible there's something here?"

Gary looked clueless.

"Gary what was special about this room?"

"This used to be Fenton's office."

"Fenton? The expert? The explosives expert?"

"Yes."

I started twisting my hands, but the ties were on tight. "You got a knife on you?"

"I have one hidden in a calf rig. But how are we going to get to it?"

I started looking around the room.

In one corner was a locked drawer.

"That has to be it," I said.

"What?"

"That looks like a safe. Its untouched, not broken. Jason must have noticed that."

"I guess..."

"Gary, my brother doesn't do anything without thinking about it at least a million times."

"Okay, but we still need to get out of these," Gary gestured to the ties.

I twisted my hands once more. "I have a plan."

Saying that, I twisted in my chair and shook it as hard as possible, until it toppled over to one side. "Ow!" I cried when I hit the floor on my head. " That fucking hurt!"

It took me a while to come back to my senses after that awful hit. I started moving closer to Gary, using the floor to propel me. The chair was digging into Gary from all sides as I tried to recover the knife, unseen. Gary started guiding me, and pretty soon I was in control of the knife. I used it first to cut my hands free, and that took a while but it happened. I used my free hands to release my legs and proceeded to free Gary.

"What now?" Gary asked.

I walked up to the drawer. "It's locked."

"Give me the knife," Gary said, so I gave it to him. He thrust the sharp end into the keyhole and started moving his hand in a strange, rapid motion.

He was trying to break the lock.

But despite Gary's efforts, the lock didn't budge.

I dropped to the floor in despair.

"We're dead, we're fucking DEAD."

19
COLTON

"Maybe there's nothing here," Gary said. "Maybe Jason has some plan of his own and is working on that as we speak."

"It can't be coincidence!"

And that's when I had another idea.

"Gary, you saw the men taking over," I said. "Did you see if anyone was holding onto keys? They have the keys for this whole place, they must have keys for this thing."

"I saw Dave," Gary said. "He was carrying them."

"Dave?"

I fumbled through my pocket and brought out the key ring I had confiscated from Dave while getting out of that room. I showed them to Gary. "Was this it?"

Gary took them from my hand. "I think so."

He started trying each one of them, sticking them inside the lock, turning but every time he failed we were both disappointed. "I don't understand," Gary said, throwing me the keys and I caught them. "Nothing works!"

I grabbed the keys and tried again.

One. Two. Three. Four.

One by one the keys lost.

Until one got stuck.

I moved it to try and get it out so I could try the other keys but the lock clicked and the drawer opened. Gary and I both stood speechless, staring at the contents.

"I'm not an expert, Gary, but that looks like a lot of C4," I said.

"It is, sir. It is a *lot* of C4 indeed."

"What's this?" I picked up a cell phone placed next to the explosives. I was about to dial when Gary stopped me.

"Be careful with that!" Gary yelled.

"Why?"

"Sir, this is the cell phone that Fenton rigged the charges with."

"I thought the charges were self-detonating."

"We thought so too," he said. "But clearly your brother and Fenton had other plans."

"So, basically I'm holding the fate of this building and everyone in it?"

"Pretty much, sir." Gary said. "The question is, what're you going to do with it?"

20

JASON

"Jason you're not just wasting my time, are you?"

I pretended to work at the charges in the basement. "No, Devyn. I'm waiting."

Devyn grabbed me and shook me. "Waiting for what?"

There was the sound of an explosion and the earth seemed to quake.

I grinned. "That."

21

JASON

"In my hand I have a cell phone," Colton said. "I press *one* button, *one*, mind you, and this whole place turns to pulp."

He could be a hard ass sometimes but I was so damn proud of that kid.

"Now, there is one other option," Colton continued. "You give me my brother and all the other captives. You let us walk. And I'll make sure no one gets hurt."

Devyn grabbed hold of a guard and asked him what was going on and he didn't sound happy about it. The guard told him what I already knew. Colton and Gary had just detonated a bomb in the fourth wing. It wasn't bad enough to hurt a lot of people but it did the job. It rattled them enough and forced them out of their holes.

Devyn came to me and pushed me towards the clearing where Colton was standing. I looked around and saw no sign of the others. Fuck. This was supposed to bring them out. Why weren't they standing among the crowd that had gathered?

"Your brother's safe," Devyn said. "Hand me the phone and I'll let you walk."

"No deal," Colton said. "You give us the captives. Or I blow this fucking thing up!"

Good boy.

Devyn turned to me. "Was there ever a threat from the charges in the basement?"

"Not really," I said, grinning.

Devyn looked like he wanted to hurt me but he did nothing.

I knew Nate was in the building. Devyn would never be that concerned about a bunch of guards or even his friends. He was treading lightly. Smart man.

"I'll handle the release of the captives," Devyn said at last. "You make sure your brother keeps his end of the deal."

I walked up to Colton and I could have hugged him but I didn't. I grabbed a gun from one of the guards and he said nothing. It was all going according to plan, but more than that, I was happy. Colton was on my side. Maybe I had misjudged him. Maybe he was our father's son after all. I stood next to him and Gary smiled at me.

Devyn was back momentarily.

Each one of the captives was with him.

Their men were still larger in number and they still surrounded us but no one risked coming close to the remote. Or either of us. The men silently joined us, and suddenly I felt stronger. I felt like I could do anything in the world. Jump from tall buildings or take down an entire army. With Colton and Gary and all these men who had stuck by us all through this, I would be stronger than I had ever been. I wish I could tell Colton how I felt. But of course there would be time for that later. *Or not. You could both die in this miserable torture chamber, along with the rest.*

I turned my attention to Devyn. "Your men have been returned," he said. "Give me the phone, Colton."

"How do we know you're not going to attack us, the minute I hand you the phone?" Colton asked. Devyn was clearly biting his tongue.

He turned to his guards. "Let them through," he said. "No one is going to so much as touch them, you hear me? Or there will be consequences. Let them leave. Stand aside. No one will use their weapons."

"Better yet," I said. "Hand your weapons to my men." I gestured to them. The men took the cue and started confiscating weapons from the guards. Pretty soon, we were equipped with an army again and in control of the situation.

When we were almost out of their reach, Colton held up the phone. "Think fast!"

Devyn lunged forward and caught the phone in his hand but he had to go on the dirt-covered ground to do it. It must have scraped him pretty bad. "Goodbye, Devyn."

We ran.

22

JASON

My legs were giving up.

"How much further?"

Colton placed a hand over his eyes.

He was searching for something in the distance. "Gary, its time."

I looked at them both, no idea what they were talking about.

"What's going on, Colton?"

Colton was still trying to catch his breath from all that running. "The phone I gave them," he said. "It was just a decoy."

He stooped and reached for his calf, lowered his sock and took out a similar phone. He stood and showed it to me. "This is the phone Fenton rigged to the charges in the cottage."

"Colton..."

"I thought about it," he began. "Devyn had all the chances in the world to do the right thing. But he kept fucking up. They all did. Dave... he..."

"Dave?" I asked. "What did Dave do?"

Colton shook his head. "It's not important," he said. "He fucked us. Betrayed us. You were right, Jason. I should have been more assertive. I should have been stronger. You were right." He paused and turned to me. "And don't get me wrong, I was pissed at you too. I was pissed that I wasn't enough for you. I was starting to think maybe I need to be with someone who cares about being with me more than some fucked up revenge plan, but I was wrong. This world, it's fucked up. And you have to be fucked up to survive."

I knew for a fact I wasn't going to let my brother become the monster that I had become.

I wasn't going to let him pull that trigger.

He wasn't going to have a hundred people on his conscience.

There was no way...

"Colton, listen to me. Forget about all this," I said. "Forget about what I said, I was being dumb. You know what I realized, when I was mourning your death? I realized that I fucked up. That I should have taken your offer and left for Europe. I should have done that because being with you is more important than anything but I couldn't do it, because I was just so angry." I paused. "But you were gone, Colton. And all I had was silence. Emptiness. I don't ever want to feel that way again. I dragged you into this mess. I always did and I was wrong."

There were tears in Colton's eyes.

His fingers hovered over the button on the phone, the same one that would launch a series of bombs inside that building. That would blow every last one of our enemies up in smoke. But what would it do to my brother?

I couldn't let this happen.

"Colton, you need to—"

I did nothing but watch as Colton's finger pressed on the button and in another minute there was a loud bang that reverberated through the forest for several minutes. There were flames and smoke in the distance, too far to hurt us physically.

There was no sign of defeat on Colton's face.

There wasn't triumph either, but it was something else—

Power.

The same high I had felt not long ago.

The same high I had wanted to keep feeling for the rest of my life.

The same high that now scared me when I saw it on my brother.

"Sir, we have to keep going," Gary said, and gestured to the men to start walking again. Colton was looking at me as though asking if I was in or out. I realized that army wasn't mine. It was his. This win wasn't mine, it was his. It wasn't me that Gary had called 'sir.'

"Are you coming?" Colton asked.

I had no choice. "Yeah."

We resumed our run.

THE END